Sienna Bailey and the Case of the Lost Locket

By
Nicole S. Palmer

Copyright © 2023 Delnic Media
All rights reserved. No parts of this publication may be reproduced, distributed, or transmitted in any form or by any means, including photocopying, recording, or other electronic or mechanical methods, without the prior written permission of the publisher, except in the case of brief quotations embodied in critical reviews and certain other noncommercial uses permitted by copyright law. For permission requests, write to the publisher, addressed "Attention: Permissions Coordinator," at the email address that follows: info@delnic.org.

Dedication

To my dear Mumma from your loving Boonoonoonoos pickney.

Acknowledgment

To my real home away from home, with which none of this labor of love would have been possible. Jamaica, land I love, you are never far from my thoughts and forever in my heart.

And to my dearest husband, for daring me to dream and sharing this journey with me. Without you, I am ordinary, with you, I am extraordinary and together, we are unstoppable.

1

It was another radiant morning at Serenity Sands, the bed and breakfast that was a gem of Montego Bay. As the sun ascended higher in the sky, its rays tenderly kissed the turquoise Caribbean waters, setting it aflame with golden and azure hues. The air was rich with the scents of freshly baked goods from Lily's oven, intermingling with the alluring aroma of traditional Jamaican spices. It was as if the morning was announcing itself, not just with light but with an entire sensory experience. Guests, who had been enchanted by the island's natural allure, began to wake and greet the new day, lending the B&B a pulsating energy that filled its charming spaces.

Under the sprawling branches of a venerable breadfruit tree, Sienna Bailey sat serenely. Her platinum blonde locs, which fell just past her shoulders, glinted in the dappled sunlight, reflecting a myriad of colors. She was engrossed in the morning edition of *The Gleaner*, her eyes scanning articles and headlines, always on the lookout for unsolved mysteries and whispered secrets of the island. Around her, the vibrant life of the B&B buzzed like a well-orchestrated symphony. Soft reggae music played in the background, providing a melodic undercurrent to the cacophony of sounds—children laughing, tourists chatting, and birds singing—that defined her environment.

Meanwhile, in the culinary heart of Serenity Sands, Lily Bailey was the epitome of youthful exuberance. Dressed in a colorful apron, her skin exuded a warm, honeyed glow under the kitchen's overhead lights. Flour was dusted liberally over her hands and even a bit on her nose, as she navigated the chaos with a skillful elegance only she possessed. Her laugh, her chatter with the kitchen staff, her concentration while kneading the dough; everything about her resonated with a life-affirming energy that seemed to uplift everyone around her.

"Sienna!" Lily's voice broke through the morning air, a call that was both urgent and filled with familial warmth. "Mi need yuh fi come taste dis!"

Abandoning her newspaper without a second thought, Sienna stood up, stretching her limbs as she made her way to the kitchen. Her eyes, a remarkable shade of hazel, surveyed the room, taking in the whirlwind of activities. Her innate curiosity was palpable, an essential trait that had both blessed and complicated her life.

"Waah gwaan, Li?" Sienna responded, her patois as natural as the air she breathed, a linguistic homage to her Jamaican roots.

Lily was already prepared, holding a spoon towards Sienna that had a generous scoop of a colorful tropical jam. "Mi waan yuh fi try dis new ting mi a cook up. Mi tinkin' it might be di next big hit pon di menu."

Intrigued, Sienna accepted the spoon, her taste buds already tingling in anticipation. As the flavors burst onto her palate—sweet, tangy, and utterly exotic—her eyes closed for a moment, savoring the experience. "Mmm, dis is heavenly, Li. Di guests gonna go wild fi dis one."

The sheer delight in Lily's eyes could have lit up the entire kitchen. "Ah, yuh like it? Dat mek mi day, Sis."

The exchange, simple as it was, embodied the essence of their sisterly relationship. Two paths diverging, yet forever interwoven by the unbreakable threads of family love and a mutual devotion to their island home.

Lily's voice grew softer, almost hesitant, as she questioned, "Sienna, yuh find any new mystery fi solve?"

Pausing, Sienna turned to look at her sister, her smile imbued with a gentleness that could only come from kinship. "Montego Bay never short pon mysteries, Li. Always sump'n new fi figure out."

Lily shook her head, her chuckle tinged with incredulity. "Mi still cyaan understand how yuh get so caught up in all a dat. But, if it mek yuh happy, dat's wat matta."

Sienna nodded in agreement, her smile steadfast, "Exactly, Li, exactly."

As Sienna exited the warm embrace of the kitchen and ventured back into the larger world of Serenity Sands, she couldn't shake off a sense of contentment. It was like walking between two worlds: one where her family, largely unaware of the depth of her interests, offered love and the comfort of a shared life; and another where she pursued her own righteous quests for justice.

Once again, Sienna melted back into the cadence of her daily life, an intriguing juxtaposition that perfectly embodied her. Above her, the Jamaican sky stretched endlessly, mirroring the complexity and wonder of the life she led, a life as intricate and compelling as the mysteries she was so determined to unravel.

2

As Sienna emerged from the aromatic haven of the bustling kitchen, her gaze was immediately drawn across the stone-tiled courtyard, which was teeming with tourists and locals alike. Seated regally on a handcrafted wicker chair, encircled by an audience of enamored guests, was Grace Bailey, the indomitable matriarch of the family. She was weaving her magic as she always did—a fusion of effortless charisma and genuine island warmth. Her laughter, robust and free, rang out over the hubbub, cutting through the myriad conversations and melding seamlessly with the ambient sounds of Serenity Sands.

The sight of her mother filled Sienna with a medley of emotions—love, respect, and a thread of anxiety that always seemed to surface when she contemplated her diverging path in life. Grace had envisioned a future where her daughters would lovingly perpetuate the legacy of the family-owned B&B, a dream that Marley and

Lily seemed more than willing to fulfill. Sienna, though, was in a state of inner turmoil. She cherished the B&B, adored its vibrant mix of people, and even loved the kaleidoscope of experiences it offered. Yet, her soul was irrevocably committed to the adrenaline-fueled world of investigations and solving crime.

Gathering herself, Sienna navigated her way through the small crowd of guests, smiling and exchanging brief pleasantries before reaching her mother. "Mornin', Mumma," she greeted softly, a touch of hesitancy in her voice.

Grace's face lit up instantly, her eyes twinkling like the Caribbean waters at high noon. "Ah, mi sweet Boonoonoonoos," she responded, her voice a symphony of warmth and love, steeped in a rich Jamaican accent. "Mi notice yuh been in di kitchen this marning. Yuh finally tinking fi mek it a more permanent arrangement?"

Sienna couldn't help but laugh at her mother's none-too-subtle attempt to steer her toward the family enterprise. Though Grace had always been skeptical of Sienna's investigative pursuits, referring to them as "fanciful hobbies," she never missed a chance to gently nudge her daughter in what she considered the "right" direction.

"Ah, Mumma," Sienna said, her voice layered with a blend of amusement and fond exasperation. "Mi was jus givin' Li a hand, yuh know how she love fi mek up new recipes. She cyaan resist tryin' out ar latest culinary ideas, an' mi couldn't se no."

Grace's eyes shimmered with a knowing wisdom, a look that suggested she saw far more than she let on. "Tru, tru. But don't forget, yuh av a place right ere inna dis kitchen too. Yuh av talent that go beyond jus sleuthin' around."

Sienna felt a familiar tightening in her gut. She adored cooking, that was true, but it was a love born from tradition and family, not vocational commitment. Her family, still laboring under the misconception that she held a culinary arts degree, expected her to eventually embrace the family business. She had dodged their questions and sidestepped confrontations, but the looming truth was a ticking time bomb.

"Mumma, yuh know how much mi treasure this place," Sienna started cautiously, as if treading on a fragile surface. "But mi also av dis odda part of me, this love fi unraveling mysteries. It nuh jus a hobby, Mumma. It a sump'n deeper. It—"

Grace cut her off, her voice tinged with a gravity that commanded attention. "Mi understand, mi darlin'. It a yuh passion. But listen well, Sienna. Dis home, our B&B, it will always be yuh sanctuary. We will always be ere fi yuh."

Sienna nodded, swallowing hard as she felt the unspoken weight of her secret bear down upon her. "Mi know dat, Mumma. And mi grateful, really I am."

Just as their intense exchange seemed to reach an emotional crescendo, a group of guests approached Grace. Eager to shower her with compliments about the delightful breakfast and the charming atmosphere, they effectively ended the mother-daughter conversation. Sienna took it as her cue to step back, allowing her mother to return to her role as the effervescent hostess.

As she retreated, Sienna felt an acute stab of guilt accompanied by an overwhelming flood of affection for her family and their idyllic establishment. Nestled amid the endless beauty of Montego Bay, Serenity Sands was a microcosm of her own life—filled with familial obligations, clandestine pursuits, and untold secrets.

With that realization, Sienna took a deep breath, immersing herself once more into other part of kher life—a life that defied conventional norms and danced to its own complex rhythm. It was a life fraught with contradictions and challenges, yet uniquely hers. And as she lost herself in the unfolding events of yet another unpredictable day, Sienna felt a heady mixture of fear, excitement, and an undeniable sense of being exactly where she needed to be.

3

Sienna reclined languidly in her hammock, cocooned by the dappled shadows of the overhanging breadfruit trees. It was a secluded corner of Serenity Sands, the family B&B, a refuge from the incessant medley of tourist chatter, clinking dishes, and the ever-present hum of reggae music. The branches of the breadfruit tree seemed to bow gracefully over her, creating a verdant sanctuary where the afternoon sun pirouetted through the leaves, painting a mosaic of light and shade. She had just picked up her crumpled copy of *The Gleaner*, the ink slightly smudged from her earlier perusal, when her focus was breached by the intrusion of a familiar voice.

"Miss Sienna, could mi bother yuh fi a moment?"

Lifting her eyes from the paper, she saw Darren, one of the stalwart cooks from their B&B kitchen, looming at the periphery of her shaded enclave. A burly man in his late forties, Darren was an embodiment of lifelong toil and passion for his craft. His dark skin was slick with a sheen of perspiration, betraying the morning's labor in the sweltering kitchen. His eyes, pools of warm brown that mirrored the rich hues of Jamaican soil, were tinged with an unusual cocktail of both anxiety and tentative hope.

"Of course, Darren! Mi happy fi help. Wah deh pon yuh mind?" Sienna greeted warmly, laying the newspaper down, her curiosity piqued.

His large feet shuffled awkwardly on the gravel as he ventured closer, his hands nervously wringing the hem of his stained apron. "Mi hear yuh help people sometime, solve di kinda problem dat di police too busy or too lazy fi look into."

Sienna tried to mask her surprise at the ask. She always tried to keep her detective work under wraps, partly to maintain its effectiveness and partly to avoid alarming her family. Yet, it wasn't entirely shocking that rumors had permeated the tight-knit social fabric of Serenity Sands, where news traveled faster than the ocean tide. She offered Darren a calm, reassuring smile. "Mi do wat mi cyan to help, Darren. Nuh worry, yuh can speak freely deh yah. A wha deh trouble yuh so?"

Darren hesitated for a moment, his hands unconsciously gripping his apron as if seeking some sort of emotional anchor. "Is mi granny's locket, Miss Sienna. It gaan. Police, dem brush mi off, say it jus los. But mi know mi heart, mi know mi didn't jus lose it. Dat locket been in mi family fi so many years, so many generations. It nuh trinket dis; mi feel she it av a piece of mi soul."

Sienna felt a tug of empathy knotting her stomach as Darren unveiled his dilemma. Family heirlooms like these were not mere material possessions; they were temporal bridges to ancestors and histories, filled with irreplaceabled sentimental value. "Can yuh describe di locket fi mi? Wen an' where yuh did seet laas?"

Gathering himself, Darren delved into the specifics. The locket was an exquisite piece, crafted with incredible attention to detail. It was made of gold, lovingly molded into the shape of a heart. Inside the heart were miniature portraits of his grandparents, a keepsake of everlasting love. The last time he had seen it, it was safely ensconced in an ornate wooden box that sat on his bedside table, a box that had now become its empty shrine.

As she absorbed Darren's narrative, Sienna felt her analytical faculties kicking into high gear. The locket wasn't merely a vanished object—it was a vanishing piece of a lineage, a family memento that had been irreparably torn. She gave Darren her word, vowing to marshal her investigative abilities to trace the locket's whereabouts.

A palpable sense of relief washed over Darren's face as he thanked her profusely before lumbering back towards the kitchen, the air around him seemingly lightened by hope.

Sienna found herself alone once more in her leafy sanctuary, but her mind was anything but idle. It was already percolating with the outlines of a plan, tinged with speculative questions and potential avenues of inquiry. While this was far removed from her more dramatic adventures—there were no missing persons to locate, no dangerous criminals to apprehend—the simple, heartfelt quest for a lost locket was, in many ways, just as compelling.

As the sun commenced its descent toward the horizon, casting ever-lengthening shadows that seemed to dance in a slow ballet over the sandy pathways and thatched roofs of Serenity Sands, Sienna felt a flame of resolve ignite within her. The idyllic tableau before her—the ceaseless waves of the Caribbean Sea tenderly kissing the sun-baked shores of Montego Bay—felt like a metaphor for her own relentless pursuit of the truth.

Just as the tides would never tire of caressing the land, so too would Sienna remain unyielding in her quest to unravel the enigma of the missing locket, until every last stone was unturned.

4

No sooner had Darren's receding figure vanished around the corner of the B&B, Sienna's ears picked up the subtle rustle of footsteps on the gravel pathway. The figure that emerged from behind the luscious fronds of a nearby palm tree was unmistakably Terrence, another employee at Serenity Sands, and a childhood friend—or frenemy, depending on the day.

Terrence was the epitome of natural allure. Tall and lean, his physique was a sculpted testament to years of outdoor activity and athletic endeavor. His eyes were the color of the clearest Caribbean waters on a sunny day, sparkling with a vivaciousness that could captivate anyone who looked into them. And that smile—effortlessly enchanting—completed the magnetic portrait, making him the center of female attention wherever he went.

But Sienna knew the man behind the magnetic facade. She and Terrence had a shared history that spanned decades, growing up as neighbors in Montego Bay. Their childhood was an endless summer of sandcastle competitions, daredevil races across the stretch of sun-kissed beach, and many an adventurous climb up the very breadfruit trees where she sat—the ones that now provided Sienna her refuge. Terrence had always played the gallant prince to a gaggle of young girls charmed by his good looks and swagger. But Sienna had been the exception, the lone damsel decidedly unimpressed by his bravado.

"Miss Sienna, mi hear seh yuh tek on yet anodda one ah dem cases?" Terrence drawled languidly, leaning back against one of the breadfruit trees with an ease that seemed almost disrespectful to the weight of the situation. A cheeky grin was stretched across his face, and it was obvious he found the whole ordeal amusing.

Sienna looked up, her eyes narrowing slightly as she observed his cocky posture. "Yes, Terrence, mi av taken on anodda case. An' what exactly yuh find so hilarious 'bout dat?" she replied, her tone tinged with a palpable irritation.

His laughter was rich and hearty, filling the air with a buoyancy that clashed jarringly with Sienna's focused mindset. "Mi jus' find it endearing, yuh know? Like yuh a act out some kind a Nancy Drew fantasy. But dis ah real life, Sienna. Ah real problems, real dangers."

The dismissive undertone of Terrence's comment rankled Sienna. His words echoed the sentiments of many others in the community who trivialized her detective ambitions, painting them as child's play or female whimsy. It was a mindset she found not just archaic, but deeply frustrating.

Not willing to let Terrence undermine her resolve, Sienna shot back, "Terrence, dis a real as it gets. People av real problems dey cyaan solve demselves, and if mi cyan help, mi a go help. So if yuh done wid yuh amusement mi av serious wuk ahead."

Terrence chuckled, his laugh resounding through the courtyard as if it were a special performance just for her. But his eyes locked onto hers, and for a fleeting moment, they flickered with something—respect, maybe, or perhaps a new level of understanding. "Yuh truly something else, Sienna. Yuh neva change," he conceded before slowly sauntering off, leaving her enveloped in her solitude once again.

Sienna watched his retreating figure, her eyes involuntarily rolling heavenwards. Yes, Terrence was a looker, but his ego seemed to consume more space than the sprawling acreage of Serenity Sands. With a shake of her head, she forcibly ejected him from her thoughts, refocusing her mental energy on the task at hand—Darren's missing locket.

As she settled back into her thought process, she felt a renewed sense of purpose envelop her, pushing aside the vexing reverberations of Terrence's laughter. As the setting Caribbean sun drenched the horizon in intoxicating shades of orange, magenta, and deep purple, Sienna felt reaffirmed in her love for her detective work. Whether it was finding missing jewelry or solving complex mysteries, each case was a chance to positively impact someone's life in a way that most deemed trivial or insignificant. And regardless of what Terrence or anyone else thought, that made all the difference in the world to her.

Unknown to Sienna, Terrence had paused in his departure and was observing her from a discreet distance. His default mischievous grin had morphed into an expression more subdued, even contemplative. For all his jest and bravado, he couldn't completely dismiss the earnestness in Sienna's eyes or the determination that so naturally adorned her countenance. Although he'd never say it aloud, certainly not to her, something about Sienna's unyielding spirit intrigued him. It offered a glimpse into a layer of her personality that he rarely acknowledged but couldn't quite ignore—a layer that made her different, interesting, and dare he think it, inspiring.

5

Just as Sienna was about to gather the various notes, photographs, and pieces of evidence to retreat to her cottage that housed her makeshift office—a room filled with corkboards, strings connecting clues, and scribbled timelines—the sound of a voice, robust and familiar, punctured her focused concentration. "Sienna!"

The timbre of the voice caused her heart to hitch in her chest. The voice belonged to none other than her father, lovingly known as Puppa by his children. A towering figure in her life, he was also the esteemed head chef at Serenity Sands. In many ways, he was the very foundation of their family, his culinary skills matched only by his wisdom and innate ability to lead.

"Hurry yuhself, mi daughta, yuh late," Puppa's voice reverberated with a kind of stern love, as he emerged from the entrance of the main house that also served as the B&B's restaurant. His tall silhouette was defined sharply against the soft glow of the sinking sun, casting long, stretching shadows across the courtyard. His locks, weathered by age and specked with strands of grey, were swept back and tucked neatly behind his ears. His face, lined with years of experience and hard work, was a blend of warm affection and lingering disappointment.

Realizing her oversight, Sienna sprung from her hammock with a jolt, leaving behind her copy of *The Gleaner* and her notepad haphazardly scattered beside it. She had completely forgotten— today was the day Puppa was to teach her his famous oxtail recipe. It was a recipe that was a closely guarded family secret, passed down through generations; it had a magical blend of spices and a tantalizing, slow-cooked tenderness that had captivated countless taste buds. The plan was for her to be the chef's apprentice for the day, another stepping stone towards inheriting the culinary reigns.

"Puppa, mi truly sorry," Sienna stammered, feeling her cheeks flush with a mix of embarrassment and regret as she approached him. "Mi got wrapped up in..."

She halted mid-sentence, her eyes locking with his. She knew she couldn't bring herself to mention "work"—her detective work, that is. Puppa viewed her sleuthing pursuits as a mere hobby, a distraction from her "true" calling. He had big dreams of her inheriting the restaurant, of her hands taking over the instruments of his trade and continuing the culinary legacy that he had built from scratch.

"...some errands," she hastily substituted, hoping he'd overlook the vagueness of her explanation.

Puppa scrutinized her face intently, his arms folded across his sturdy chest. Those eyes, so much like her own, were not easily deceived. "Yuh seem to be gettin' caught up in a lot ah dem 'errands' lately, Sienna. Ah di errands more important than learning the family tradishun, the skills dat mek us who we are?"

A knot of tension tightened in her stomach, turning into an uncomfortable lump. She loathed lying to Puppa, but she also knew that he could never fully comprehend her aspirations, steeped as he was in traditional values and the legacy of lineage. To him, the idea that she might want to own and operate a detective agency was as foreign as snow in Montego Bay.

"Mi beg yuh, forgive mi, Puppa. Mi will mek sure to be present and fully engaged for di next lesson. Just give mi a lickle more time to settle some tings," Sienna pleaded, her eyes imploring him to understand, to give her the freedom to explore her true calling.

With a heavy sigh, Puppa's stern gaze softened, and he ran his large, callused hand through his dreads. Sienna knew this gesture well; it was his tell, his way of signaling he was wrestling with concerns he didn't quite know how to express. "Sienna, mi love yuh, an' mi want wat's best fi yuh, but yuh cyaan keep avoiding yuh responsibilities and yuh heritage."

His words were like boulders, settling between them with a weight that couldn't be easily moved. "Mi unnastand, Puppa," Sienna murmured softly, feeling the impact of every syllable.

As she watched her father turn and stride back towards the kitchen, the hub of his world, a deluge of emotions swept over her. She was caught in the crossfire of her individual desires and the collective dreams of her family. Yet as her eyes drifted back to her forsaken *Gleaner* and her thoughts circled back to Darren's desperate request, she knew where her soul was anchored. Her path might not align with the expectations of her lineage, but it was undeniably her own path, and she felt compelled to follow it.

The Caribbean sun, by now a fiery orb flirting with the horizon, cast a golden luminescence over the entire landscape. It illuminated the looming choices and inevitable confrontations that lay ahead of her. Her passion for solving mysteries, for stepping into the complications of other people's lives to offer aid, was not something she could simply set aside. This passion was as much a part of her identity as the culinary arts were a part of her family's legacy. It was a dual heritage she had yet to reconcile, but one she could no longer afford to ignore.

6

With the golden sun still proudly asserting its position in the azure Jamaican sky, Sienna took her leave from the cacophonous activity of the B&B kitchen—a space pulsating with the clatter of pots and pans, the sizzle of spices, and Puppa's robust commands. She made her way to her personal sanctuary, a secluded cottage situated in a tucked-away corner of the family property. Shielded from the laughter and chatter of the guests and far enough from the kitchen to escape the hypnotic aroma of traditional Jamaican cuisine, it was her fortress of solitude. This space allowed her to delve into the shadowy recesses of her second life: her work as a burgeoning private investigator.

Her makeshift office was nothing short of organized chaos. At the center of the room stood a wooden desk overflowing with a smorgasbord of paperwork that appeared discordant at first glance. Tucked among invoices from food suppliers and upcoming menus that her father had asked her to review, were the objects of her true passion: her confidential case files. Today, these secretive documents were intermingled with handwritten notes, photographs, and newspaper clippings, evidence of her tireless commitment to her investigative endeavors.

Eager to shed the role of sous-chef and reluctant heir to the family business, Sienna hastily unfastened her apron and hung it on the back of her chair. She then reached for her well-worn notepad, its pages filled with hastily scribbled observations and questions. It contained all that she had jotted down during her clandestine conversation with Darren, a young man whose desperation was as palpable as the tropical heat. His grandmother's locket, a valuable family heirloom adorned with intricate designs, had inexplicably disappeared following a soiree at Serenity Sands. The case was nebulous, lacking any concrete evidence or immediate leads; what remained were a smattering of potential witnesses, individuals who might unknowingly possess fragments of this increasingly complex jigsaw puzzle.

She seated herself, took a deep, meditative breath to center her thoughts, and began to meticulously construct a timeline of the unfolding drama. The event at the epicenter was the party—an effervescent gathering teeming with B&B guests, local friends, and the various staff members of Serenity Sands. Darren had been there, the locket gleaming proudly around his neck. Then came the jarring reality of the morning after; the locket was nowhere to be found. What followed was a frenzied and ultimately fruitless search that only amplified Darren's despair and urgency.

Turning her attention to the list of names Darren had rattled off, Sienna began to categorize the potential suspects. Jerome was the town's jeweler, an affable but opportunistic man with a discerning eye for precious items. Susie, the diligent maid who had cleaned Darren's room after the revelry had subsided, was another name worth probing. Last but not least was Leon, a close friend of Darren's, who had not been shy about openly admiring the locket during the party itself. Each individual presented unique avenues for inquiry, subtle leads that could potentially spiral into revelations.

Sienna surveyed her accumulated notes with the scrutinizing eye of a seasoned detective. She only had a few precious hours before the curtain of dusk enveloped Montego Bay, but it was ample time to initiate her inquiries, perhaps even elicit a confession or stumble upon a hidden clue. This required a deft touch; she needed to reconcile her identity as a discreet investigator with her more public role as an indispensable part of the B&B staff, the chosen heiress to the

Serenity Sands empire. Her mission was to crack this case wide open, all while maintaining a facade that would prevent her family from discovering her true calling.

Finally, steeling herself for the complex web of conversations and interrogations that lay ahead, Sienna took one last comprehensive look at her notes. Her eyes skimmed over her scribbled hypotheses, lingering momentarily on the list of potential suspects. The bustling streets of Montego Bay were her next destination, a living tapestry teeming with secrets, clues, and half-told truths. But as Sienna readied herself to walk this tightrope of duality, she was acutely aware that she was undertaking a journey that transcended the singular quest for a lost heirloom. Each step she took on this investigative path was also a step towards carving out her own destiny—a journey away from the familiar yet limiting environment of her father's kitchen and deeper into the labyrinthine corridors of her own aspirations and dreams.

7

As the sun dipped low, casting an orange glow over the horizon, Sienna found herself stepping into the bustling streets of Montego Bay. Her first destination was the iconic Jerome's Jewelry, a quaint little shop that had been a fixture in the community for decades. Amidst the cacophony of vibrant local businesses, Jerome's stood out, a testament to its reputation for fine craftsmanship.

Jerome was a local legend. Petite in stature but not in character, he wore delicate spectacles that sat precariously on the edge of his nose. Behind those glasses were eyes that sparkled with the same enthusiasm as the jewels he masterfully worked with. Inherited from his father, the shop had become a Montego Bay landmark over the years. It was celebrated not only for its high-quality jewelry but also for Jerome's unparalleled ability to assess the true value of various pieces brought into the shop.

As Sienna entered the space, the gentle chime of a bell announced her presence. Jerome, deeply engrossed in inspecting a piece of jewelry under a magnifying lens, looked up and straightened his posture immediately. His face broke into a warm, welcoming smile as he greeted her.

"Ah, Sienna! Wah mek yuh drop by? Yuh inna di mood fi buy sump'n special?"

Feeling her detective instincts kick in, Sienna quickly formed a plan. "Jerome, yuh rememba Darren, mi bredren? Him lose him Granny gold locket an' mi a wonda if it mighta reach yah. Yuh cud tek a gander inna yuh stock?"

Jerome's eyes widened momentarily before he nodded and vanished into the depths of his shop. Sienna used the opportunity to carefully scrutinize the space. She observed Jerome from her vantage point, and although his demeanor seemed innocent enough, she reminded herself that she needed concrete evidence to confirm any theories.

Emerging from the back room, Jerome returned with a face tinged with genuine disappointment. "Mi real sorry, Sienna. Mi nuh find nuh locket weh match wah yuh a talk 'bout."

Before she left the store, Sienna tossed out a final, casual question. "Oh, an' Jerome, yuh did roll up at Serenity Sands fi di big bash di odda night?"

Jerome chuckled as he adjusted his glasses. "Dem kinda bashment? Nah, mi love. Mi too ole fi dat kinda ting. Mi rather cozy up wid a book."

Thanking him one more time, Sienna stepped back into the deepening dusk. The air was thick with the sounds of life: laughter, chatter, and the distant call of the ocean waves. Jerome had seemed honest, but her detective's intuition told her she had much more to uncover.

As the colors of the evening sky shifted from the warmth of sunset to the cooler shades of twilight, Sienna moved through the energetic streets, her thoughts turning towards her next lead. Her footsteps directed her back to Serenity Sands, where she would have another conversation—this time with Susie, the maid who had been tasked with cleaning Darren's room. The sun might have set, but for Sienna, the investigation was far from over.

8

Susie was as much a part of the B&B as the beautifully carved mahogany furniture that adorned its rooms. A stout woman with skin as dark and shiny as the seed of the Ackee fruit, her hair was neatly braided and often adorned with Hibiscus flowers. Her voice, melodious as the cooing of the yellow-billed cuckoo, was a familiar comfort to the guests and staff alike. She had been working as a maid at the B&B for the last fifteen years, and over the years, she had become part of the B&B family.

As Sienna entered the bustling dining hall, the delicious aroma of jerk chicken, freshly baked breadfruit, and sweet sorrel wafted through the air. She saw her father, his tall frame bent over the stove, the light from the kitchen casting a warm glow around him. Her sisters, busy serving the guests, laughed and chatted amongst themselves. In the midst of all this was Susie, humming a tune as she cleaned a table, her movements as fluid as the rhythm of the reggae music playing softly in the background.

Choosing her moment carefully, Sienna approached Susie, taking a seat at the table she was cleaning. "Evenin', Susie," she greeted the older woman with a smile.

"Sienna, mi dear, how yuh doing?" Susie responded, her face lighting up at seeing the young woman.

"Mi gud, tanks. Mi did need yuh help with sump'n though," Sienna started, trying to sound casual. "Mi friend, Darren, him lost a gold locket him granny gave him. Him tink seh him lost it here, di night of di big bash. Yuh didn't happen to find anyting while yuh did clean up, did yuh?"

Susie paused, leaning against the table as she thought. "Mi nuh 'member seeing anyting unusual when mi did clean," she responded after a moment. "But, it was a large crowd, an' people lose tings all ah di time. Mi wi check di lost an found fi yuh."

Sienna nodded, thanking Susie. The older woman bustled away, leaving Sienna alone at the table, her thoughts running in circles. As she got up to leave, she glanced around the dining hall, her eyes catching a momentary glimpse of her reflection in a mirror on the wall. Amidst the warm, welcoming glow of her family's B&B, she was the secret detective, solving mysteries, chasing leads. It was a thrilling thought, and Sienna couldn't help but smile.

9

Sienna's steps slowed as she navigated through the grand hall, adorned with antique furniture and vibrant artworks. The warm glow of the chandeliers above reflected off the polished floor, giving the space an air of elegance. Just as she turned a corner, she nearly collided with Marley. Quick reflexes on both sides prevented an accident, but the tension was palpable.

Standing tall and commanding, Marley was the epitome of grace and authority. She was the eldest of the siblings, her skin a rich cocoa hue that shimmered in the soft lighting. Unlike Sienna's blonde dreadlocks, Marley's hair was as dark as the night sky, meticulously gathered in a high bun that exuded professionalism. Her sharp, almond-shaped eyes scanned everything in their path, missing absolutely nothing and assessing all they beheld.

Marley had wasted no time stepping into their parents' shoes. Right after completing her education, she had fully committed to the family's bed and breakfast. Now, she managed the day-to-day operations with a balance of strictness and efficiency. She was not just passionate about the B&B; she was its beating heart, being meticulously groomed to take over the reins from their parents in due course.

"Lawd, mi almost knock yuh down," Sienna exclaimed, clutching her chest as her heart pounded.

Marley's eyes narrowed instantly. "A yuh fault, Sienna. Yuh need fi pay attention to weh yuh a go, instead of moving around like yuh lost," she retorted, her words as crisp as a freshly laundered sheet.

Suppressing a sigh, Sienna took a deep, grounding breath. "Mi have a lot pon mi mind, Marley. Mi a juggle nuff tings," she defended.

Marley raised an eyebrow skeptically. "Like what, pray tell? Yuh little detective game? Cause mi nuh see yuh putting in enough work 'round here to justify yuh gallivanting."

Sienna felt a sting at Marley's words. Her sister had always viewed her investigative pursuits as trivial, nothing more than child's play compared to the high-stakes reality of running a family business.

"Mi contribute inna mi own way, Marley," Sienna retorted, frustration creeping into her voice.

Exhaling loudly, Marley rolled her eyes. "Listen, Sienna, mi love yuh, but yuh need to hear this: yuh detective hobby a just a sidetrack. We have a family business fi run, an' it high time yuh start taking dat seriously. A weh Mumma and Puppa expect."

Sienna's lower lip quivered as she bit it softly, trying to maintain her composure. "Marley, mi just nuh ready fi commit mi whole life to di B&B," she confessed. "Mi need space to explore, to find out who Sienna really is and weh she want."

Shaking her head as if disappointed by a child's naive understanding, Marley looked at her sister with a blend of concern and disbelief. "Yuh nuh a pickney no more, Sienna. Yuh need to face di music an' grow up."

Without waiting for Sienna's response, Marley spun on her heels and marched away, her steps echoing in the grand hallway. Sienna was left standing there, alone and weighted down by a complex web of emotions and the heavy silence that filled the space. The words that had been left unsaid between them seemed to hang in the air, a silent testament to the emotional gulf that had widened once more.

10

Sienna felt like a ship lost at sea, tossed about by waves of doubt and uncertainty, but she knew exactly where to find safe harbor: in Auntie Faye's comforting presence. Tucked away in a cozy corner of the family's expansive B&B property was Auntie Faye's enchanting cottage. The quaint structure was more than just a home; it was a sanctuary filled with memories of countless conversations, empathetic advice, and laughter that melted stress away. If Sienna had to pick one consistent, grounding presence in her life, it would undoubtedly be Auntie Faye.

Faye was her mother's younger sister but embodied a spirit that was remarkably different from her sibling—a spirit that drew Sienna irresistibly closer, much like a moth to a gentle flame. Faye was grace and vivacity personified. Her skin was as warm and rich as freshly brewed cocoa, lined with the wisdom of her years and always glowing with an infectious smile. Her hair, a voluminous cascade of silver curls, framed her face like a halo and was often playfully contained by vibrant scarves. The wrinkles around her eyes, which would flare up with her frequent laughter, were less marks of aging and more badges of her jovial nature. Her rounded figure, softened by years and experience, radiated an embrace even before she physically extended her arms.

Although she functioned as the front desk manager for the B&B, her charming personality allowed her to be so much more. She was the epitome of Jamaican hospitality, greeting guests with a warmth that made them feel like they were part of the family. But in Sienna's life, Auntie Faye played an even more significant role. She was the confidante, the wisdom-giver, and most crucially, the keeper of Sienna's biggest secret—her true academic background and aspirations.

As Sienna gently pushed open the door of the cottage, her senses were immediately engulfed by the soothing aroma of fresh ginger tea, which carried a subtle undertone of aromatic pimento. Auntie Faye sat nestled in her favorite rattan chair, her eyes traveling through the pages of a book that had clearly been read and re-read many times over. Her eyes lifted, and a loving smile graced her lips. "Come sit down, mi love," she gestured, patting the cushioned seat next to her invitingly.

Her eyes softened further as they fell upon Sienna's red, teary eyes and drooping shoulders. "Ah wah happen, mi darling?" she inquired softly, her voice acting as a salve on Sienna's turbulent emotions.

Sienna let out a heavy sigh, sinking into the chair. "Ah Marley, Auntie. She jus' nuh understand why mi nuh ready fi commit mi whole self to di family business. She say mi detective pursuits a jus' a childish diversion an' mi nuh really contributing."

Faye extended her hand, enveloping Sienna's in a gentle, reassuring grip.

"Listen mi love, Marley might seem hard, but deep down, she worry 'bout yuh. She have her way ah seeing tings, true, but dat nuh mean she nuh care."

Nodding, Sienna bit her lip, contemplating her next words carefully. "Auntie, mi feel like a deceiver. Mi never really go school fi learn 'bout culinary arts. Mi education was all 'bout criminology, and mi feel like mi haffi tell dem."

Faye looked into Sienna's eyes, and her own sparkled like twin stars, shining with understanding and unconditional love. "Sienna, mi have always known. Yuh haffi follow yuh own path, not walk on one laid out by oddas. Yuh haffi be true to who yuh are."

Tears welled up in Sienna's eyes as she absorbed Auntie Faye's words. "But, Auntie, what if dem nuh understand? What if dem think mi a jus' waste time an' potential?"

A tender smile spread across Auntie Faye's face. "Well then, yuh just have to prove them wrong, mi love. Show dem yuh capabilities. Show dem yuh nuh just daydreaming but yuh can mek this hobby into a real career. Show di world di real Sienna—one who nuh only strong, but also ambitious and destined for greatness."

Embracing Auntie Faye tightly, Sienna felt a newfound resolve filling her. She knew she had someone to lean on, someone who believed in her even when she doubted herself. And now, strengthened by Auntie Faye's wisdom and love, she understood that it was time to be open and honest with her family. It was time for Sienna to show them, and perhaps even herself, the incredible person she was meant to be.

11

Just as Sienna felt a sense of comfort and affirmation after her conversation with Auntie Faye, she found herself again in turbulent waters. The grand hall, usually a place of warmth and family memories, had turned into an arena for familial conflict. Standing strategically between Sienna and her path to her office was Marley, like a gatekeeper questioning her credentials. The air was heavy with unspoken words and bottled-up emotions. Marley's gaze was like an anchor, pulling Sienna down into a sea of responsibilities and expectations.

Physically, Marley was an imposing figure. She stood tall, with a frame that was both wiry and robust—much like the bamboo trees that lined the periphery of the B&B property. Her skin, rich and dark, took on a special glow in the dimming twilight. Her eyes, a unique shade of hazel gifted from their paternal grandmother, bore into Sienna with unyielding scrutiny. Her dreadlocks, unlike Sienna's freely flowing locs, were groomed meticulously and styled into a tight bun, symbolizing her rigid approach to life.

"Sienna," Marley broke the silence, her voice unyielding and stern, "Mi need fi chat wid yuh. Mi nuh want nuh interruption."

Sienna sighed deeply, her shoulders drooping, "Ah wah now, Marley? We jus' had ah talk. Wah more yuh wan' seh?"

"Is not 'wah more'," Marley retorted sharply, her arms crossing her chest defensively. "Ah how long yuh tink yuh cyan go on like dis? Di B&B ah not some playground."

"Mi nuh see di problem," Sienna shot back, her voice tinged with defensiveness. "Mi balance mi responsibilities here wid mi detective wuk. It's not like mi a neglect anyting."

"Balance? Yuh call dat balance?" Marley scoffed, her voice rising in both volume and pitch. "While mi an' Lilly deh yah full-time, a carry di heavy load, yuh just float in an' out. Dat nuh fair, Sienna."

Sienna, stung by the criticism, tried to justify herself. "Marley, mi do mi part. Mi handle mi shifts, mi deal wid di guests, mi even help wid di paperwork. Yuh act like mi nuh contribute nuhting!"

Marley's eyes narrowed, her jaw clenching as she considered Sienna's words. "Sienna, yuh nuh get it. We family. Dis business is our legacy. It need all ah we, not just part-time help. Yuh cyaan be half-in, half-out."

Sienna's eyes softened, her voice laden with emotional vulnerability. "Mi understand dat, Marley. But mi also haffi be true to miself. Mi nuh tink it fair fi sacrifice all mi dreams an' ambitions fi di family business."

"Ah suh yuh see it?" Marley's voice took on a softer, almost sorrowful tone. "Yuh see yuh dreams as more important than our family's legacy? Ah what our parents built, our grandparents built. Yuh willing fi throw dat away?"

Sienna took a deep breath, her voice shaky. "Mi nuh throw it away, Marley. Mi jus' add sump'n else to it. Mi love our family. But mi need mi own path too."

Marley let out a long, heavy sigh, her body language signaling a grudging acceptance. "Alright, Sienna. Mi may not agree, but mi hope yuh know wah yuh a give up. Ah better be worth it, dis 'hobby' of yours."

With that, Marley turned and walked away, each step echoing in the grand hall. Sienna remained there for a moment, taking in the gravity of what had just unfolded. The challenge of her chosen path loomed large, magnified by Marley's skepticism. The burden of proving herself, both as a worthy family member and as a detective, was now twofold. Her thoughts were a chaotic whirlwind as she finally continued her journey towards her sanctuary: her office.

12

Situated on the far reaches of the B&B's lush property, obscured by foliage and the serenity of nature, sat Sienna's makeshift cottage that served the dual purpose of being her office and her personal sanctuary. The structure, which had started its life as an oversized tool shed, had undergone a miraculous transformation. It had been crafted meticulously into a unique space that not only mirrored Sienna's multifaceted personality but also resonated with her deep sense of connection to her Jamaican heritage. It was as if the modest wooden structure had absorbed the essence of Sienna herself, as its walls were adorned with elements that ranged from vibrant Caribbean motifs to cryptic symbols that referenced her love for mystery and investigative work.

When you walked in, the first thing that struck you was the cozy yet chaotic living space that welcomed guests. Eclectic pieces of furniture, each with their own history and story to tell, filled the room. These were items that Sienna had salvaged and repurposed, much like the clues she pieced together in her detective work. Hanging on the walls were a mix of local artwork, framed photographs, and even a few awards she had won for solving minor local crimes. The atmosphere was palpable, a heady blend of Jamaican culture and the undying allure of unsolved mysteries, creating an almost mystical energy that danced in the air.

The ground floor was predominantly her workspace and one couldn't help but feel a sense of awe at the palpable intensity of her commitment to her vocation. Anchoring the space was a medium-sized desk made of reclaimed wood, a second-hand gem that Sienna had personally refurbished. Papers were strewn about, intermixed with sticky notes written in her scrawling handwriting and an assortment of writing utensils ranging from ballpoint pens to vintage fountain pens. Adjacent to the organized chaos of her desk stood a large cork-board, which was currently vacant but had seen its share of case notes, photographs, and leads pinned onto its surface in a web of crime-solving intricacies.

Sienna's laptop sat in the center of the desk like a throne for the technological soul of her enterprise. It was flanked by a carefully curated collection of criminology textbooks, detective novels, and notebooks filled with her own observations and theories. These were her silent mentors, her trusted companions in a trade that often required her to walk the path alone. Near the window was a small shelf housing various camera equipment and GPS devices, essentials for her fieldwork, making the room an amateur detective's dream.

Adjacent to her desk area, segregated by a low wooden divider, was what she affectionately referred to as her "mini lab." It was an organized mess of forensic equipment, microscopes, test tubes, and beakers, a stark contrast to what one would expect to find in a Jamaican hideaway. Yet, the space was quintessentially Sienna, a corner where science met curiosity. She had even installed a small darkroom setup for processing her own photographs, offering her complete autonomy over her investigative procedures.

On the opposite side of the room, beneath a mezzanine level reached by a spiraling iron staircase, was a cozy corner that was the antithesis of her lab. This corner boasted a large, plush armchair and a vintage floor lamp that cast a warm, inviting glow. Here, Sienna often found solace, sinking into the cushiony depths of her chair as she sipped on aromatic Blue Mountain coffee and pieced together the jigsaw puzzles of her cases. Many nights, this very corner had been her solitary retreat, the soft buzzing of the lamp offering silent company as she delved into the realms of the unknown.

Above this ground-floor amalgamation of work and wonder was a loft that served as Sienna's private sleeping quarters, accessible via a steep, narrow wooden staircase that was tucked discreetly into the corner of the room.

This loft was intimate, just spacious enough to accommodate her modest bed, encased in white mosquito netting that shimmered ethereally in the moonlight. A small but quaint bedside table stood next to it, often holding a book she was currently engrossed in and a cup of herbal tea. The most breathtaking feature of this loft, however, was its glass enclosure. With floor-to-ceiling windows, Sienna had an unfiltered view of the natural beauty that surrounded her—from the lush greenery of the property to the endless expanse of the Caribbean Sea.

The loft's ceiling was more skylight than roof, a design specifically tailored to Sienna's love for the night sky. On clear nights, she would lie on her bed, lost in the grandeur of the universe, as constellations played hide and seek amongst the celestial tapestry. The rhythm of the ocean waves crashing against the shore served as her nightly lullaby, while the salty sea breeze, wafting in through the open windows, was her natural sedative. It was her cocoon of serenity, a place where her thoughts could drift freely, unshackled by the demands and judgments of the outside world.

Sienna's cottage was a universe unto itself—a realm where her love for the complexities of human behavior collided with her deep-rooted ties to her Jamaican upbringing. It was a sanctuary that encapsulated her dreams, her hopes, and her uniquely distinct identity. As she prepared to delve into her newest case—the enigmatic disappearance of a family heirloom locket—Sienna couldn't help but feel a rush of exhilaration. Her recent confrontation with Marley had indeed left emotional scars, but Sienna was a resilient soul. As she booted up her laptop and arranged her notes, she knew she was stepping onto a path that had the power to redefine her life in ways she had yet to imagine.

13

The first tendrils of dawn began to etch their presence into the dark sky, casting a palette of soft pinks and fiery oranges across the horizon. Sienna stirred gently in her bed, the subtle sound of crashing waves in the distance serenading her awake. The scent of the sea mingled with the crisp morning air that floated in through the open windows, embracing her senses in a natural wake-up call. Sliding her feet onto the cool wooden floor, she donned a thin, cotton robe over her nightgown, securing the belt as she made her way down the narrow, wooden staircase that led from her private loft to the main area of her cottage-turned-office.

Upon descending, her eyes took a moment to adjust to the muted lighting of the room, which was still bathed in the ethereal glow of the waning moonlight. It cast mysterious shadows on her workspace, adding an aura of intrigue to the objects that cluttered her desk. Notes, scribbled hastily on scraps of paper; transcripts from interviews; an array of black and white photographs; maps of various scales with pins and colored strings marking places of interest—each a clue in a grander narrative that had begun to consume her existence. Sienna breathed deeply, savoring the lingering scent of last night's coffee, adjusted her glasses with a sense of determination, and prepared to delve headfirst into the labyrinthine mystery that awaited her.

Time seemed to dissolve as she immersed herself in the investigation. The fresh scent of morning was gradually replaced by the invigorating aroma of freshly brewed Blue Mountain coffee, its robust scent chasing away the final remnants of sleepiness that fogged her mind. With each passing hour, her focus tightened around the emerging patterns she was beginning to discern within the chaos of information before her. She scoured every transcript, dissected each photograph, and overlaid maps, her eyes darting between different pieces of the puzzle. Her mind was abuzz, a cacophonous orchestra of analytical reasoning, deductive logic, and intuitive leaps. And while the pieces of the puzzle were aligning, forming preliminary shapes of suspects, locations, and motives, the complete picture remained an enigma, lurking just beyond the grasp of her comprehension.

Suddenly, her gaze landed on the wristwatch that sat beside a cup of now-lukewarm coffee. The realization that time had flown jolted her back to reality. It was time to momentarily abandon her detective persona and transition back to her familial role as assistant chef at the family's B&B. With a sense of resignation, she meticulously stacked her case notes, archived the digital files on her laptop, and covered her board of clues with a black cloth, as if tucking away her detective self until it could re-emerge later under the cover of darkness.

Making her way through the garden path that connected her personal sanctuary to the sprawling manor house, Sienna entered the large, bustling kitchen. It was as if she had stepped into another world—a world of sound, aroma, and kinetic energy that stood in stark contrast to the reflective solitude of her office. Pots and pans clanged, stovetops hissed, and knives struck cutting boards in a rhythmic cadence.

Her father, affectionately known as Puppa, was the anchor in this storm of culinary activity. His imposing figure moved effortlessly through the organized chaos, his hands deftly slicing, stirring, and seasoning as he orchestrated the morning's breakfast offerings. His deep, melodious voice was the soundtrack of the kitchen—a seamless blend of cooking instructions, anecdotes, and hearty laughter that filled the air with a sense of comforting warmth.

The kitchen staff, a quartet of individuals who had served the family for multiple generations, buzzed around Puppa with the synchronicity of celestial bodies orbiting a sun. The line between employee and extended family had blurred over the years, making for an atmosphere of mutual respect and familiarity that was palpable to any onlooker.

Amidst the bustling staff was Lily, Sienna's effervescent younger sister. Like a daisy in full bloom amidst a field of green, her youthful energy injected a different kind of life into the room. She was preoccupied with assembling a selection of pastries, her hands coated in a fine layer of flour. Her laughter danced through the kitchen, punctuating the air with pockets of youthful exuberance. Occasionally, she would catch Sienna's eye, offering a smile of encouragement and understanding, her gaze seeming to penetrate the weight of thoughts Sienna carried with her.

But conspicuously missing from this scene was Marley, Sienna's older sister. The air seemed to grow slightly heavier with her absence, as though the room could sense the unresolved tension between the siblings. Memories of their recent confrontation crept into Sienna's mind, an unwelcome specter she couldn't quite shake off, despite the otherwise jovial surroundings. Yet, for now, she chose to set it aside, concentrating on the culinary duties that demanded her attention.

As the hours slipped away, Sienna surrendered to the repetitive yet comforting acts of chopping vegetables, stirring sauces, and carefully monitoring ovens. The rich aromas of jerk chicken, freshly baked bread, and exotic spices filled the room, enveloping her in a sensory bubble that temporarily drowned out her concerns about the missing locket and the case that continued to gnaw at her thoughts. For the moment, she was Sienna, the devoted daughter and assistant chef, her detective alter ego safely tucked away in the cloak of her office. Yet, even as she reveled in the olfactory symphony of Jamaican cuisine, a part of her yearned for the enigmatic allure of the mystery that awaited her return.

14

As Sienna pushed open the ornate wrought-iron gates of Serenity Sands, her family's bed-and-breakfast, the atmosphere around her shifted palpably. She found herself plunged into the cacophonous tapestry that was Montego Bay at high noon. Her goal for the afternoon was to navigate through the heart of the city, a populous residential area framed by the pulsating Gloucester Avenue— affectionately dubbed the 'Hip Strip' by locals and tourists alike. Her aim was to seek out Leon, a name that had surfaced multiple times during her investigation and now represented a potential lead in her ongoing case.

Walking through the animated streets, the city seemed to reach out and envelop Sienna in a rich tapestry of sensory experiences. It was as though Montego Bay was a living, breathing entity, its very core pulsating with an infectious energy that you could not help but absorb. Every corner of St. James Street's sprawling marketplace was abuzz with the chatter of vendors, each attempting to outdo the others by shouting the allure of their wares with unparalleled fervor. A veritable cornucopia of stalls flaunted vibrant arrays of fruits, spices, and freshly prepared food. The scent in the air was a heady blend of olfactory notes—smoky wafts of jerk chicken fresh off the grill, the tropical sweetness of ripening mangoes, and the tangy, peppery aroma of spices. This symphony of sensations was complemented by the distant growl of car engines negotiating the congested roads, the punctuated honks of motorists navigating through bottlenecks, the hypnotic rhythms of reggae music that wafted from a hole-in-the-wall record store, and the energetic intermingling of local voices conversing in a blend of English and Jamaican Patois.

As Sienna wove her way further into the city and neared the area where Leon resided, the bustling noises of commerce and entertainment began to fade. They were replaced by the more mundane yet equally poignant sounds that characterized the city's residential neighborhoods—the laughter of children who had commandeered the streets for a lively game of football, or soccer as it is known in other parts of the world.

The melodic calls of indigenous birds as they darted between the red and orange blossoms of flamboyant trees; the rhythmic creaking of clotheslines straining under the weight of damp laundry flapping in the breeze; and the low hum of radios broadcasting local news and music from within the homes that lined the streets. Sienna felt her senses absorb this part of Montego Bay, a version not often caught by the lens of a tourist's camera, but very much the authentic soul of the city—a living, breathing entity with its own distinctive rhythm and pace.

Reaching the end of a narrow, cobbled lane, Sienna found herself standing before a small house painted in hues that rivaled a tropical sunset. Leon, her target, was a laid-back individual in his late twenties who possessed a physicality that spoke of laborious work, the product of years employed at the local dockyard. His skin had absorbed the Caribbean sun to a rich shade of mahogany, and his dreadlocks were arranged in a neat fashion, pulled back away from his face. What caught Sienna's attention the most were his eyes—an unusual shade of green that held an inexplicable twinkle, as if he were perpetually amused. His clothing was simple yet striking, comprised of a well-loved pair of jeans and a vivid red T-shirt that boldly proclaimed 'One Love.'

Meeting her eyes, Leon grinned broadly and greeted, "Wah gwaan, Sienna? Mi neva expect fi see yuh 'round 'ere."

Striving to maintain a casual air, Sienna responded, "Mi jus' a pass through, Leon. Mi did a wonda if yuh could ansa some questions 'bout di party las' week."

For a moment, the mirth in Leon's eyes flickered, replaced by a momentary look of suspicion. However, he shrugged it off and reclined deeper into his porch chair, creating an atmosphere that encouraged a deeper conversation. Overhead, the Caribbean sun blazed relentlessly in the clear sky, casting sharp shadows across Leon's yard, and the sounds of Montego Bay continued to narrate a complex symphony in the background.

As they began to delve into the particulars surrounding the inexplicable disappearance of the mysterious locket, Sienna sensed that she was inching closer to solving a puzzle that had held her in its grasp for weeks. But with each revelation, each unveiled layer, the complexity of the situation seemed to deepen, its web becoming more convoluted and intricate. Yet Sienna was not one to be easily dissuaded. Challenges were the lifeblood of her work, and she embraced them wholeheartedly. As the sun started its descent toward the horizon, casting a warm, golden hue over the bustling streets of Montego Bay, Sienna felt an invigorated sense of purpose. She was more than ready to pull at the tangled threads of this perplexing mystery, unraveling it clue by clue until the truth lay bare before her.

In the quiet corner of his porch, under the soft hum of the ceiling fan, Leon leaned back in his chair. He scratched at his bearded chin, his eyes thoughtful. "Mi rememba di party, Sienna. 'Twas a lively one dat. Full a good vibes an' irie people."

Sienna nodded, her pen ready to jot down any potential leads. "Yes, it was. But mi more interested 'bout afta di party, Leon. Did yuh see or hear anyting unusual? Anyting 'bout Darren's locket?"

Leon shifted in his chair, his eyes wandering to the children playing in the street. "Mi cyaan say mi did, Sienna. Di party did loud an' everyone was enjoyin' demselves. If sometin' ah gwan, mi neva notice."

Sienna pressed on, "What 'bout afta di party? A wen it wind don? Yuh rememba seein' Darren? Or di locket?"

Leon was quiet for a moment, his eyes narrowed in thought. "Mi... mi rememba seein' Darren 'round midnight. 'Im was a bit tipsy, laughin' wid some guests. 'Im locket? Mi nah sure. But now dat yuh mention it, mi tink 'im did still 'ave it 'round 'im neck."

Sienna jotted this down, her mind buzzing with potential leads. The timeline was starting to take shape, but there were still many unanswered questions. "Tank yuh, Leon. Yuh 'ave been a big help."

Leon shrugged, a slight grin on his face. "Mi glad fi help, Sienna. Mi hope yuh find dat locket. 'Tis a shame when tings like dis go missin'."

15

As Sienna stepped off Leon's wooden porch, her heels softly clicking against the cobblestones as she started her trek back to Serenity Sands, a fresh spark ignited in her. Each step felt like a march towards clarity in unraveling the enigma of the missing locket. Yet, as she glanced back to see the sun dipping below Montego Bay's horizon, painting the sky with shades of crimson and orange, she knew her journey was far from its conclusion. The intricate web of clues, the differing accounts of events, they weighed on her like a novelist's unfinished manuscript. With the kaleidoscope of city noises becoming fainter as she walked further away, a mental list began to form in her mind—leads that still needed chasing, questions yearning for answers, and a night that promised little sleep but much discovery.

By the time she was halfway to her destination, Montego Bay had transitioned into its languid afternoon persona. The morning's bustling market activities had dissipated, now replaced by the tranquil resonance of the city in its midday phase. A delectable blend of scents filled the air around her. The robust aroma of jerk chicken, suffused with an intoxicating mix of spices, wafted past her, blending seamlessly with the sweeter smells of ripe mangoes and coconuts from roadside vendors. From a distance, she could make out the distinct, rhythmic bass of reggae music emanating from a dancehall, setting the tempo for the city's pulse.

Montego Bay was an incredible swirl of diverse cultures, its rich tapestry woven from variegated threads of humanity. But today, Sienna found it difficult to lose herself in the city's multifaceted beauty. Her mind was still tethered to the room she had just left, where Leon's steadfast gaze and honest tone had put forth a version of events at odds with Darren's narrative. A dissonance that would not easily be settled had introduced itself into the equation.

The specific details of the locket's last-known whereabouts were rapidly becoming a maze of contradictions. Darren had been unequivocal: he'd last seen his cherished locket during the festivities of the much-discussed party. But Leon's story painted a vastly different picture, one where Darren had conspicuously donned the piece of jewelry well after the party had ended. These diverging accounts couldn't be easily dismissed—they introduced a rift into the story that demanded resolution.

As Sienna digested these complexities, her footfalls grew faster, almost involuntarily. The cobblestone streets underneath her became a blurry carpet as she maneuvered effortlessly through the pedestrian crowds. Her heartbeat seemed to synchronize with her accelerating pace, each thump a resounding question mark echoing in her chest: If Darren had been dishonest, was it a mere slip of memory, or did his deception mask a darker intent?

Nearing Serenity Sands, she saw the tall, swaying palm trees that acted like gatekeepers to her temporary abode. The gentle, rhythmic sounds of the Caribbean Sea intensified, synchronizing with the soft, natural rustle of the sea grape leaves in the wind. The bed and breakfast, an architectural remnant of colonial times, stood resplendent against the scenic backdrop of the beach. The waning sunlight kissed its coral-painted walls, setting them aflame in a golden aura. She noticed the darkened outlines of guests as they mingled on the veranda, their laughter and conversations merely wisps carried by the evening wind.

Entering the estate's courtyard, Sienna couldn't help but marvel at the garden that was alive with the dazzling hues of purple and red bougainvilleas in full bloom. But tonight, this slice of paradise felt like it had been transformed. What was typically a sanctuary now seemed like a theater where the next act of her unfolding drama could take place—a stage set with clues and characters, each holding a piece of the elusive truth she sought.

Pausing outside the staff lounge, her heart felt like a drum in her chest, its beat quick and irregular. The evening wind made the palm leaves dance, their long, graceful shadows mimicking the movements on the lounge's veranda. Though muffled, she could hear the familiar sounds that usually spelled 'home': the clatter of kitchen utensils, the sizzle and pop of spices in hot oil, the deep timbre of her father's laughter. But on this particular night, those sounds felt far away, almost as if they belonged to another dimension— one where life was simple and answers were straightforward.

Taking a deep breath to steady herself, Sienna pushed open the door. The staff lounge came into view, an open space that somehow felt fraught with the electricity of impending revelation. Scanning the room for Darren, she was imbued with a sense that she stood on the edge of an epiphany—one that could shatter previous misconceptions and propel her investigation into uncharted territories.

16

In the warm, inviting ambiance of the staff lounge, Sienna's eyes landed on Darren. He was reclined in a worn armchair, his posture a blend of exhaustion and apprehension. His dark eyes seemed a swirl of emotion, each glance containing multitudes that words could not express. His thumb idly moved back and forth over the well-worn fabric of his uniform shirt, a gesture that betrayed his anxiety. Darren was not a man of great wealth, and from the stories he'd told Sienna, it was clear that his grandmother's locket was invaluable to him—not just in monetary terms but in emotional and sentimental worth as well.

Taking a step forward, Sienna felt a renewed sense of resolve rise within her. The atmosphere seemed to thicken, each second magnifying the gravity of the moment. "Darren," she broke the silence, her voice carrying both the comfort of familiarity and the firmness of intent. The sound of his name seemed to startle him, his eyes widening for a split second before regaining their composure.

"Sienna," he echoed softly, his feet touching the floor as he rose from the armchair, his expression transforming into something far more opaque, something that Sienna couldn't immediately decipher.

"A jus' talk to Leon," she continued cautiously, her eyes never leaving Darren's face. His body language shifted subtly, muscles tensing for a moment, and she noticed a spark of confusion replace the surprise that had been there moments ago. "Him seh dat after di party, him see yuh wearing yuh granny's locket. But yuh tell mi seh yuh last see it in yuh locker dat very day."

A puzzling array of emotions danced across Darren's face, his eyes darting as if trying to catch invisible fragments of truth in the air. "But mi... dat nuh...," he stuttered, his words stumbling over themselves like river stones caught in a sudden deluge.

Composed but vigilant, Sienna pressed on. "Yuh did say dat when yuh a work, yuh always keep di locket locked away inna yuh locker. Mi correct, nuh?"

Darren nodded hesitantly, his gaze meandering from the ground, tracing an invisible line back up to meet Sienna's eyes. "Yeah, mi did say dat, but..."

Sienna inhaled deeply, steadying herself. The weight of this moment was palpable; it was a tipping point in her quest for the truth, a precarious balance of uncertainty and revelation that hinged on their conversation. A quiet tension spread across the room, filling the corners and crevices with a tangible sense of expectation. She studied Darren closely, observing as his eyes flickered, fingers absently toying with his shirt hem. Overhead, the fluorescent lights offered no warmth, only elongating the shadows that fell across his face, exaggerating the lines of worry etched into his features.

"Darren, listen to mi," Sienna's voice softened but retained its urgent edge. "Mi need fi know what really happen. Something nuh add up right, yuh see mi? Mi want to help yuh, but mi can only do dat if mi get di full story, di real story from yuh."

Drawing in a shaky breath, Darren's gaze briefly escaped through the window, capturing glimpses of the tranquil world outside before reluctantly returning to the moment. For what felt like an eternity, he seemed to grapple with his thoughts, the room filled only by the distant murmur of life going on elsewhere in the B&B and the slow, rhythmic ticking of the wall clock.

"Sienna, mi really nuh too sure anymore," he finally admitted, his voice almost drowned out by his own uncertainty. "Di night... it get kinda blurry. Mi drink more than mi shoulda, so mi memory nuh all dat clear."

Empathy filled Sienna's eyes; the realization struck her that Darren himself seemed entangled in his own foggy recollections. The mystery surrounding the locket had revealed itself to be far more complicated than she had originally anticipated.

"Mi understand yuh situation, Darren," Sienna responded, compassion flavoring her words. "Mi know seh times hard for yuh. But mi still believe inna yuh. An' mi gwan do mi best to sort dis all out."

A glimmer of gratitude replaced the cloud of confusion in Darren's eyes. "Tanks, Sienna," he whispered, the corners of his mouth turning upward in a small, fragile smile.

As Sienna left the confines of the staff lounge, her thoughts were a swirling maelstrom of possibilities and theories. The story had fissures, inconsistencies that had added new dimensions to the mystery. It was like navigating through a labyrinth shrouded in fog, but her resolve remained unshaken.

The pieces of the puzzle were slowly coming together in her mind.

With a newfound determination, Sienna outlined her next steps. She knew she would have to dig deeper, talk to the other members of the staff who had been present both at the B&B and during the night of the eventful party. She would have to scrutinize Darren's locker as well, seeking any overlooked clue that might shed light on the puzzle. The locket was not merely an ornament; it was a treasure trove of family history and cherished memories, and it could not remain unaccounted for. She had to find it, and she was resolute in that pursuit.

However, she made a conscious decision not to confront Darren about his locker just yet. She'd give him some breathing room, make him more comfortable before prying further. Timing was everything, and she would choose the perfect moment to ask about his locker, ideally before his next shift ended. This would be the next critical juncture in her ongoing investigation, and Sienna was more than ready to tackle it.

17

The tropical sun was descending, its orange hues casting a serene glow over Montego Bay—a stark contrast to the turmoil that churned within Sienna. The route back to the staff lounge was one she had tread many times, but today, every step felt different. The atmosphere seemed charged, pulsating with the intensity of her newfound mission to solve the lingering mystery of the missing locket.

Sienna had always considered the staff lounge at Serenity Sands a sanctuary amidst the chaos of the bustling bed and breakfast. Framed by a large window, the golden sunlight spilling in had a way of bathing the room in a soft, inviting glow. The walls were a canvas of vibrant, locally sourced art, and the air was a harmonious medley of overlapping conversations, the clatter of utensils from the adjoining kitchenette, and the sporadic, joyous laughter that seemed to erupt from the souls of the workers.

Yet today, this sanctuary was poised to transform into an arena of confrontation. Sienna's heart thundered in her chest as she caught sight of Darren, who was seated on one of the plush couches, seemingly ensconced in the labyrinth of his thoughts. His shoulders were slouched, his eyes downcast; those dark, expressive eyes seemed to mirror a soul caught in a storm, and the shadows that lurked beneath them spoke volumes of nights robbed of sleep and days filled with an unending loop of worries.

With a hint of sternness veiling her otherwise calm demeanor, Sienna began, "Darren, mi haffi talk to yuh."

The hum of voices that had been a constant backdrop in the lounge seemed to ebb away at her words, creating an aura of palpable tension. Darren's eyes flicked upward, a complex interplay of emotions cascading across his face: surprise, confusion, and an inkling of what looked like dread.

"Mi haffi look inna yuh locker," Sienna declared, her voice resolute. The atmosphere in the room grew thick with tension, as if time itself had paused to hear Darren's response.

The initial shock that flashed through Darren's eyes morphed quickly into a look of palpable fear. "Wha...? No, Sienna, yuh cyaan do dat," he replied, his voice trembling as his hands clenched into tight fists.

"Darren, mi just waan--" Sienna began, searching for the right words to articulate her thoughts, but Darren cut her off.

"Mi seh NO, Sienna!" The words erupted from him, a whispered shout that resonated like a bolt of lightning in the suddenly too-quiet room. His eyes darted nervously around the lounge, betraying his fear that their private conversation had become public theater.

Before Sienna could gather her thoughts or muster a response, Darren sprang to his feet, his chair scraping sharply against the tiled floor as if mimicking his abrupt movements. "Mi break done. Mi haffi go," he stated, his voice tinged with urgency as he dashed out of the room.

As he left, the murmurs returned, filling the lounge like a low tide coming in, whispers and exchanged glances conveying the collective curiosity and concern of the room's occupants. The myriad questions that Darren's exit had spawned were left to hover in the air like an unsettled mist.

Darren's locker, which had initially been a small fragment of this vast puzzle, had now become a crucial focal point. It was as if the locker had transformed into a symbolic vault, holding undisclosed truths and undisclosed lies, waiting to be unsealed. But how could Sienna access it without crossing a boundary?

Outside, the sun had completed its descent, surrendering to the oncoming twilight. The once-vivid hues of the landscape were now awash in the soft, muted tones of the evening. And as the curtain of night began its descent, Sienna found herself mired in a complexity of thoughts and decisions, each one carving a deeper layer into this unfolding mystery. What had elicited such a fearful reaction from Darren? What secrets were ensconced within that locker? And what would be her next move in this intricate web of uncertainty?

18

An icy knot of tension twisted in Sienna's stomach as she watched the swing door of the staff lounge oscillate, a silent testament to Darren's hasty retreat. The whirlwind of emotions that had swirled through the room moments ago had now been replaced by an uncomfortable silence, one that resonated with the echo of unsaid words and untold secrets. Darren had disappeared into the labyrinth of the B&B, leaving behind a cloud of uncertainties that seemed to darken the room.

For a moment, Sienna stood there, her heart pounding with adrenaline, her mind racing with unanswered questions. The impulse to follow Darren, to demand the truth that he seemed to be shrouding, was overwhelming. But she held herself back, a voice of reason reminding her that the pursuit could do more harm than good. Darren was scared, that was evident. Her chasing him could just push him further into his shell. She had to be careful, tactful.

Instead, Sienna's gaze slid to the staff's locker room. The usually inconspicuous door now felt like a looming challenge. Behind it, she knew, lay Darren's locker – and perhaps, the answers to the questions that had been tormenting her. But for now, the path to it was barred, not by a physical barricade, but by the countless pairs of eyes around her. Every staff member in the room was a potential observer, their curiosity piqued by the day's unsettling events. She couldn't risk arousing further suspicion.

And so, Sienna made a decision. She would bide her time, wait for the bustling B&B to quiet down, for the staff to return to their homes and families, for the night to cast its cloak of privacy. Only then would she venture into the locker room, only then would she pry open Darren's locker. She didn't know what she was going to find, or if she would find anything at all. But she knew she had to try.

As the day drew to a close, Sienna found herself going through the motions. She helped close down the kitchen, exchanging the usual goodbyes with her family, responding mechanically to Marley's light-hearted jabs, offering Lily advice on some culinary problem. But her mind was elsewhere, ticking down the minutes until she could carry out her plan.

As the final rays of the sun dipped below the horizon, the B&B slowly began to wind down. The last of the guests retired to their rooms, the staff trickled out one by one, their wearied smiles belying the satisfaction of another successful day. The B&B, usually buzzing with life and energy, settled into a serene quiet, the only sounds being the gentle lullaby of the waves against the shore.

Finally, the moment arrived. Sienna slipped out of the main building, her heart pounding in her chest, her palms slightly clammy. She knew what she was about to do was risky, and that the stakes were high. But the potential reward was worth the risk, she convinced herself.

As she stood outside the locker room, the world around her held its breath. The usually benign door now seemed foreboding, holding behind it not just the staff's belongings, but potentially the key to unravel the mystery that had entwined itself around her life.

Taking a deep breath, Sienna reached for the door handle.

Sienna's heart pounded with anticipation as her hand settled on the cool metal of the locker room door. This space, typically filled with the lively banter and camaraderie of the staff, was eerily silent in the evening hours. She pushed the door open, revealing the empty room beyond.

Rows of lockers extended back into the dimly lit room, their uniformly grey exteriors giving nothing away. A faint scent of industrial cleaner, overlaid with the more personal scents of the staff – a hint of cologne here, the subtle aroma of a favorite shampoo there – hung in the air. Overhead, fluorescent lights cast long, indistinct shadows, flickering occasionally and adding to the room's stark ambiance.

Starting from one end, Sienna began her search. The locker numbers, etched onto small brass plaques, climbed in sequence. Each locker bore the hallmarks of its owner – a sticker here, a magnet there. Despite their uniformity, Sienna knew that behind each door lay a unique slice of someone's life – clothes, mementos, perhaps even secrets.

Sienna moved with purpose, her mind swirling with both guilt for invading personal spaces and a fierce determination to find the truth. She was well aware of the fine line she was walking, justifying it to herself as a necessary step in her quest.

Eventually, she found what she was looking for. Locker number 37. She recognized it from a friendly argument she'd overheard in the staff lounge about a month ago. Darren and another waiter, Ravi, had engaged in a playful debate over football teams. Darren, an avid supporter of the Jamaican Reggae Boyz, had displayed his loyalty by pasting a small team sticker on his locker. A small thing, but a distinctive one.

Her hand hesitated over the locker door, feeling the cold, unyielding surface beneath her fingertips. It was a small, inconspicuous object, but it held a world of possibilities. Behind this simple, metal door could be the answers she sought, the clues to put the pieces of the puzzle together.

Upon closer inspection, Sienna noticed something unusual: a padlock, its silver surface gleaming under the stark fluorescent lights, securely fastened on Darren's locker. A jolt of surprise washed over her. In all her time at the B&B, she had never known any of the staff to lock their lockers. The unspoken rule of trust and mutual respect among them deemed such precautions unnecessary. The sight of the padlock, therefore, not only deepened the mystery surrounding Darren's locker but also stirred an unsettling concern about what it might hold within.

The presence of the padlock did more than merely pique Sienna's interest. It was an anomaly, a silent yet potent indicator that something was not right, that she was on the right track. The significance of this small, seemingly insignificant object was not lost on her. Her resolve to unravel the mystery was now stronger than ever.

A soft, almost inaudible chuckle escaped Sienna's lips as she reached into her left back pocket, her fingers brushing against the familiar, reassuring shapes of her lock picking set. A set of tools she had often been ridiculed for carrying around, dismissed as a frivolous indulgence from her college days when she had surprisingly chosen an unusual elective - Safecracking 101. Little did her critics know that this so-called 'foolish' elective might just prove to be her saving grace.

She remembered the first day of class, her curiosity piqued by the strange collection of picks, tension wrenches, and rakes that the instructor had spread out on the table. Over the course of the semester, she had learned the delicate art of lock manipulation. It was a skill that required patience, precision, and a deep understanding of the complex inner workings of various locks. Every tumbler and pin, she was taught, had a role to play, and understanding their delicate dance was key to unlocking the secret they guarded.

As Sienna withdrew the tools from her pocket, she marveled at their humble yet potent functionality. They were slender, made of durable stainless steel, and each served a unique purpose. She felt a sense of calm settle over her. Her hands knew their work well, each movement practiced and sure.

Gently, almost reverently, she began to work on the padlock, her senses fully attuned to the task at hand. The world outside the locker room ceased to exist. All that mattered was the small piece of metal she was manipulating, the way it responded to her touch, and the secrets it was guarding.

The padlock finally clicked open, releasing the shackle with an almost inaudible gasp. Sienna's heart pounded in her chest as she slowly swung the locker door open, her senses alert to every detail.

At first glance, Darren's locker was a picture of chaotic disarray. Items of clothing were haphazardly strewn around, mingling with discarded food wrappers, an array of personal items, and other random detritus of a busy life. Sienna felt a slight disappointment bubble up in her chest. Was this all just about a man's struggle to keep his personal space tidy?

But then, as she started sifting through the locker's contents, her keen eyes spotted something out of place – a couple of folded, worn-out pieces of paper tucked away in a corner. She gently picked them up, her curiosity piqued.

The notes were written in a crude, forceful handwriting, the letters bold and angry. Each word seemed to have been etched into the paper with an intense, almost frantic energy. Sienna's pulse quickened as she started reading the first note. "You took something that doesn't belong to you. Give it back!" The message was simple, threatening, and left no room for misinterpretation. Whoever had written this note was angry and demanding the return of something. What could "it" be referring to?

As she unfolded the second note, a chill ran down her spine. "You're running out of time." The message was even more ominous than the first. The tone was sinister, bearing a grim sense of urgency that sent a shiver down her spine.

Sienna felt a wave of unease wash over her as she re-read the notes. The chaotic disarray of the locker no longer seemed innocuous. It was a reflection of the turmoil Darren was in, a silent testament to the fear he was living with. It was no wonder he had been so desperate to prevent her from accessing his locker.

Sienna looked around the deserted locker room, the threats inked on the pieces of paper still echoing in her mind. Darren was in trouble, and he was too afraid to seek help. But now, Sienna knew. And she was determined to not only find the lost locket but also to uncover the truth behind these threatening notes.

19

Sienna felt her heartbeat resonate in the deafening quiet of the locker room as she took her smartphone in her hands. She opened the camera app and painstakingly angled it to capture every nuance of the ominous, jagged handwriting that adorned the threatening notes she had found in Darren's locker. Every word, every stroke of the pen, was an irrevocable testament to the veiled danger that lay hidden. She took multiple shots from different angles, zooming in and out to ensure that each image was a pristine record, a digital imprint of the sinister messages that had so far remained concealed in this overlooked corner of Darren's world.

After meticulously verifying that each image was crystal clear, Sienna pivoted her focus to restoring the locker to its original state, with its unique cacophony of disorder and disarray. This operation was not just a matter of putting things back; it was an act of preserving the status quo of Darren's cluttered world. A stray, forlorn sock was carefully bent back into its original curve and replaced beside a jumble of assorted knickknacks. Crumpled pieces of paper, each carrying its own weightless significance, were pushed back beside a half-empty bottle of some generic cologne, its scent tinged with undertones of Darren's life. Finally, a well-worn cap, its fabric frayed from use, was delicately placed atop a teetering pile of magazines, their pages yellowed with age and neglect.

Satisfied with her efforts, she cautiously picked up the notes she had unearthed, refolding them along their original creases and crevices. She then placed them back in the obscure, dim corner where they had been hiding, as if patiently waiting for someone to discover them. Every movement of her hands was methodical, almost robotic, in its exactitude, as she engaged in a meticulous ballet of folding, adjusting, and returning each object to its predetermined spot. Her eyes scrutinized every inch, every angle, ensuring nothing seemed out of place, nothing would raise suspicion.

Sienna reached for the padlock that hung from the locker door. The air in the room felt viscous, laden with the gravity of her discovery and her subsequent actions. Her fingers threaded the metal shackle through the locker hole with a kind of reverence, a soft but resonant click sealing it shut. She tugged the lock twice, reassuring herself it was secure. A wry, ironic smile crossed her lips as she realized she was, in essence, locking away a secret she had just stumbled upon.

Stepping out of the locker room and into the ever-vibrant atmosphere of the bed and breakfast, Sienna was engulfed by a dissonance that seemed almost surreal. Guests' laughter echoed from the poolside, mingling with the rhythmic clatter of kitchenware as the evening meal was prepared, and the varied conversations of the staff punctuated the air. These familiar sounds, usually comforting, felt oddly out of place, like colorful patches in a tapestry that had begun to fray at its darker, hidden seams.

She walked mechanically, each step taking her closer to her makeshift office—a cozy, secluded space located in the far corner of the sprawling property. This was her sanctuary, her haven for piecing together disparate fragments of human lives into comprehensible wholes. But today, the space felt altered, constricted, as if the walls were leaning in, privy to the complexity of her current case.

Once inside, Sienna found herself surrounded by the familiar clutter that adorned her working environment: heaps of haphazardly placed papers, her detective notepad laden with scribbled observations, even the soft, comforting aroma of her favorite lavender room spray. Yet these familiar elements were now backdropped by an air thick with urgency and latent danger.

Sienna pulled out her phone once again, swiping through the gallery to the images of the notes she had just captured. Each pixel seemed to shout a warning, each line of text a riddle begging to be solved. She was standing on the precipice of an ominous abyss, peering down into its depths, both compelled and repelled by what she might find therein.

She carefully placed her phone next to her notepad, contemplating the gravity of her next moves. Each decision was a potential trigger, capable of causing a ripple effect through the myriad lives touched by this unfolding enigma. The boundaries between her responsibilities—to her family, to her business, to her role as an undercover detective, and to her staff like Darren— were becoming increasingly porous and convoluted.

Confronting Darren was risky; it could provoke defensiveness or even worsen whatever precarious situation he was ensnared in. Taking the matter to her family was equally perilous, threatening to expose her dual life as a detective, a secret she had guarded assiduously. And as for the police, without concrete evidence or a fuller understanding of the broader circumstances, their involvement could escalate matters beyond control.

Taking a deep, steadying breath, Sienna felt the weight of her situation sink in, even as she felt invigorated by the challenges that lay ahead. She was at a crucial crossroads, tasked with not only finding a lost family heirloom but also unraveling a deeper, darker tapestry of secrets and threats. With resolve solidified by the pressing need for action, Sienna reached for her notepad and began to sketch out the contours of her multi-faceted plan.

20

Sienna's small office was bathed in the soft glow of a desk lamp, casting a warm aura that contrasted sharply with the cool Jamaican night seeping through the cracks in the window. The room was filled with the gentle whir of the printer, punctuated occasionally by the distant laughter and chatter of the B&B guests, unaware of the tangled web of intrigue unfolding behind the scenes.

As the printer finished its task, Sienna carefully picked up the freshly printed photos, her fingers lightly tracing the ink as if the tactile connection might reveal more about the cryptic messages. She turned her gaze toward her cork board, a seemingly innocuous board covered by a large map of Montego Bay. Anyone who looked at it would think it a mere decorative touch, but its real purpose was far more strategic. With a practiced motion, she flipped the map over, revealing what lay behind it—a meticulously assembled crime board.

This was the epicenter of her sleuthing endeavors, a tangled web of red yarn connecting a plethora of pinned photographs, newspaper clippings, and hand-written notes. Different colored pushpins indicated various leads, persons of interest, and evidence, a physical manifestation of the labyrinthine thoughts and theories swirling in her mind.

Sienna held the printed photos in one hand and with the other, took a clear pushpin from a small container on her desk. She paused, her eyes scanning the intricate layout on the board, before choosing a vacant space near the center. It was important to place it there—a physical representation of the growing importance of this new piece of evidence in the grand puzzle she was determined to solve.

Pinning the photos carefully to the board, she took a step back. The printed threats seemed even more ominous in this context—harbingers of danger amidst an already complex case. "You took something that doesn't belong to you. Give it back!" One note read. The other was equally chilling: "You're running out of time."

They were messages of urgency, layered with an undertone of menace. Sienna pondered their implications. Were these threats specifically about the locket? Or were they indicative of another, even darker secret that Darren was harboring?

She felt a tingling sensation at the base of her skull, the rush of adrenaline that always accompanied a new clue or a significant development in her cases. The messages added another layer of complexity to the puzzle, but they also offered potential pathways to the truth. Sienna knew she needed to act quickly; time was running out, just as the note had warned.

Sienna picked up a red spool of thread from her desk drawer and cut a small length. She fastened one end to the pushpin that held Darren's picture and connected it to the new evidence. A red line, a pathway to follow, a tangible connection between Darren and this newfound layer of menace.

For a moment, she stood there, her eyes darting back and forth between the faces and clues scattered across her crime board. She thought of Darren's confusion, his reluctance to share, and now these threats. The locket, as significant as it was, might just be the tip of an iceberg, a gateway into deeper, murkier waters. It was no longer just about a missing heirloom; it was about the safety and well-being of someone who, despite his secretive demeanor, was a part of the close-knit community at Serenity Sands.

The clock on her desk indicated that it was late, way past the time anyone would consider reasonable to be up. Yet the night was Sienna's companion, a cloak of stillness that allowed her the space and tranquility to think, to connect the dots. She felt closer now, closer to an elusive truth that had been darting just out of her reach.

She glanced once more at the newly added threads and pins, a mental snapshot that would fuel her next steps. The path to the truth was convoluted, laden with obstacles and riddles, but Sienna Bailey was undeterred. A wave of determination washed over her, refreshing her weary mind like a splash of cool Caribbean water. Sienna flipped the map back over her crime board, concealing it once more from the world. It was a hidden landscape of mystery and intrigue, only to be revealed when she had gathered all the pieces of the puzzle.

Now, what was her next move? Interviewing other staff was on the list; any one of them could have pertinent information, willingly or otherwise. And then there was Darren; her intuition told her that he wasn't the type to craft these messages, but was he the recipient? Was he the victim, the perpetrator, or merely an unwitting participant in a drama yet to fully unfold?

Tugging at a strand of her hair in thought, Sienna took a deep breath. Her detective's intuition tingled with possibilities. Time was of the essence. If the threats were to be believed, something was going to happen—soon. She couldn't afford to let things unfold naturally; she needed to be the catalyst, the force that would push the dormant elements into a reaction.

Sienna sat down at her desk once more, her mind racing with plans, counterplans, and contingency routes. She pulled out a fresh sheet of paper from her notepad and began listing names—every staff member, known friends of Darren, anyone who had recently interacted with him. Next to each name, she noted down what she knew about their relationship with Darren, no matter how insignificant it seemed. She wasn't ruling out anyone, not at this stage.

As her pen moved across the paper, she felt her confidence growing. The missing locket, the inconsistent stories, the threatening notes—each was a piece of a puzzle, a single frame in a much larger, more complicated picture. With every stroke of her pen, with every connection she made on her board, Sienna felt as if she were pulling the lens back to reveal more of the scene, broadening the scope of her investigation and drawing her closer to the heart of the mystery.

Finally, after what felt like hours but was probably closer to half an hour, she leaned back in her chair, looking at the list she had compiled. Her eyes flitted back to the now carefully concealed case board, examining the space where the photos of the threatening notes lay beneath the surface, and finally back to her list. The scope of her investigation had expanded, but so had her understanding of the complex web she was navigating. The sensation was exhilarating. Here, in this room filled with her secret life, she felt more alive than ever.

She knew she was treading on dangerous ground; the more she uncovered, the riskier it became. Yet, the dangers of discovery paled in comparison to the thrill of the hunt, the intellectual high of solving the unsolvable. This was who she was, what she was born to do, and nothing—not the potential backlash, not the lurking dangers—could deter her now.

With a renewed sense of determination, Sienna grabbed her keys and phone, locking her office behind her as she stepped out into the Jamaican night. It was time to take the next step, to rattle the cage a little and see what would come flying out. She felt ready, primed for whatever challenges lay ahead. After all, this was what she lived for—each mystery was a call to adventure, and she had just picked up the phone.

And so, armed with new evidence and buoyed by an indomitable spirit, Sienna strode forth into the labyrinthine corridors of human motives and dark secrets, ready to untangle the threads of a mystery that seemed to deepen with every step she took.

21

As Sienna made her way past the corridor, a door swung open with a flourish, sending a shockwave of surprise through the corridor. "Young lady, just where do you think you're going at this time of night?" The voice that followed was deep and resonant, echoing through the wooden panels of the hallway.

Sienna couldn't help but release a soft, almost involuntary giggle. That voice could only belong to one person—Uncle Lando. In the spectrum of her life, he stood out like a lighthouse on a foggy night. His actual name was Orlando Kerr, a name that carried substantial weight on the island. He was well-known, well-respected, a certified public accountant whose reputation for meticulousness was almost as widespread as his love for jazz and vintage record collections—reggae, naturally.

As a child, Sienna had grappled with the cumbersome syllables of his name, always tripping over the sounds in youthful impatience. "Ohwrl-do," she would try, her young, lisp-carrying tongue stumbling until she'd throw her hands in the air and gleefully shout, "Uncle Lando!"

The name stuck, much to the amusement of her family and the absolute delight of the man himself. It was as if the nickname solidified their bond, carving out a unique space for the two of them within the complicated dynamics of an extended family.

And so, 'Uncle Lando' he had remained. Over the years, the name had come to mean so much more than a simple moniker; it was a title that implied trust, wisdom, and a fair share of good-hearted mischief. Uncle Lando was not just an accountant but also a repository of ancestral stories, a purveyor of sage advice, and now, Sienna's unwitting confidant in her increasingly convoluted quest for the truth.

Sienna whirled around, a playful grin on her face, she placed her index finger to her lips, gesturing for silence. Uncle Lando's eyes twinkled even more as he beckoned her into his cluttered office. Stacks of ledgers and papers sat neatly on his wooden desk, a testament to his meticulous nature as both a certified public accountant and the B&B's full-time bookkeeper.

"Ah, come in, come in," he said, reverting to his native patois as he closed the door behind her. "Wha' yuh up to, mi likkle sleuth? Ah see dat glint in yuh eye."

Sienna chuckled. "Uncle Lando, yuh too observant, yuh know."

Uncle Lando's office was a maze of ledgers, tax forms, and calculators. Yet, amidst the numerical chaos, was the ledger for the family's B&B, a testament to his other role as the establishment's bookkeeper.

Once the B&B grew in reputation, pulling in tourists and locals alike, Uncle Lando transitioned to a full-time position, devoting himself to the B&B. In this capacity, he'd become a cornerstone of the place, ensuring that the numbers added up, right down to the last cent.

Sienna took a seat across from her uncle's massive oak desk, the surface of which was cluttered with papers and trinkets that seemed disparate yet somehow connected, much like the fragments of her ongoing case. Uncle Lando leaned back in his chair, the leather creaking under his weight, and gave her that searching look that he'd mastered over the years—a look that seemed to see right through her.

"So, wha' yuh up to dis time a night, Sienna?" Uncle Lando asked, one eyebrow slightly raised, a playful undertone in his voice. "Yuh nuh usually deh 'bout at dem late hours 'less yuh on to som'ting, nuh true?"

Sienna felt a tiny smile tug at the corner of her mouth. Her uncle didn't know the full extent of her secret investigations, but he knew enough to sense that she was always up to more than met the eye. He had always shown a penchant for amateur sleuthing himself, perhaps a leftover trait from his youthful days when he'd devour detective novels like they were gospel. Over the years, he'd become a kind of sounding board for Sienna, always ready to lend an ear and perhaps a nugget or two of wisdom as she talked through her various cases with him.

"Yuh could say dat, Uncle Lando," she finally answered, her eyes meeting his. "Mi find miself inna web of confusion an' mystery, an' mi tryin' fi sort out di puzzle."

He leaned forward, resting his arms on the desk, a look of keen interest replacing his earlier playfulness. "Well, yuh know yuh always got me yah fi bounce ideas off of. Weh yuh got?"

The rapport between Sienna and Uncle Lando was like a well-oiled machine, a sacred space where ideas could be exchanged freely, and where even the most perplexing of mysteries seemed to shrink under the weight of collective scrutiny. Tonight, their impromptu meeting felt more significant than ever, an essential pit stop on her journey toward the truth. And as she began to unfurl the layers of her investigation, Sienna felt reassured by the presence of her life's most constant mentor, silently grateful for this haven in a world of ever-growing uncertainties.

"Ah've stumbled pon som' inconsistencies, Uncle Lando. Pieces nuh fit togedda yuh know? An' ah jus' find some disturbing notes in Darren's locker."

"Hmm, dat sound serious," Uncle Lando rubbed his chin thoughtfully. "An' Darren is...?"

Sienna quickly briefed him on Darren's situation, emphasizing the importance of the missing locket and how it seemed tied to family heritage.

Uncle Lando leaned back, absorbing the details. "An' yuh think Darren nuh completely honest?"

"It nuh so much dat he dishonest, but im memory blurry. An' ah find dese notes warning him 'bout som' he took dat nuh belong to him."

"Mmm, yuh should follow dis lead, Sienna. But be careful, yuh know. Di stakes dem high, especially when it come to tings like family an' heritage."

She nodded. "Ah will, Uncle Lando. Tanks fi di advice."

As she turned to leave, Uncle Lando called out, "An' Sienna?"

"Yah, Uncle?"

"Keep yuh eyes open an' yuh senses sharp. Di world nuh always as it seems, but yuh nuh need me fi tell yuh dat."

With a grateful smile, Sienna nodded and left the office, her heart a blend of warmth and resolve. Uncle Lando was right; she had to tread carefully. But the path, however twisted, would lead her to the truth. And she was more determined than ever to find it.

Nicole S. Palmer

22

As Sienna stepped through the doorway of Uncle Lando's office, the luminescence from the hallway light seemed to take on a softer, more subdued quality, as though it too was aware of the profound nature of the discussions that had just transpired. She cast a quick glance at her wristwatch, its luminous hands pointing to an hour far later than she anticipated. The ticking clock seemed to chastise her, its mechanical gestures accusing her of losing herself in a world of conjecture, deductive reasoning, and the richness of her uncle's storytelling and wisdom. Her original plan of interrogating a person of interest was derailed; whoever it was had likely retreated into the tranquil embrace of the Caribbean night, far from the confines of the B&B.

As Sienna acknowledged this, a twinge of frustration flared within her. However, she quickly quelled the emotion, setting it aside like an irrelevant clue. If she'd gleaned any wisdom from her self-taught forays into investigation, it was the indispensable role of timing. In the intricate dance of detection, timing was the choreography that either made or marred the performance. And at this late hour, her physical and mental reserves signaled their own need for a pause—a time for rest, rejuvenation, and reflection. Her cognitive landscape felt fragmented, like a complex jigsaw puzzle from which key pieces had been deliberately removed. The contours were jagged and ill-defined, rendering the full picture elusive. And to reconstruct that picture, she knew she had to operate at full capacity.

With an accepting exhale, Sienna swiveled gracefully on her heel and commenced her journey down the antique wood-paneled hallway of the bed and breakfast. The walls, rich and finely grained, seemed almost sentient in their quietude, absorbing the sound of her measured footsteps as if allowing her a ghostly, unobtrusive passage through the hushed building. Her thoughts began to drift toward her dwelling—her quaint, cottage-like shed tucked away in a secluded part of the property. The imagery of that sanctuary of solitude and peace formed in her mind like a calming balm; where the nocturnal orchestra of crickets and other night insects serenaded her solitude, and the whispering wind played softly among the palm leaves, carrying the ocean's salty kisses.

As she navigated through the expansive, foliage-draped grounds of the B&B, the Caribbean night seemed to envelop her in an almost tangible cloak of velvety darkness. Scattered lamp posts, standing like solitary sentinels along her path, projected warm oases of light onto the gravel walkway, their luminescence serving as transient guideposts among the shadows, much like stars obscured by a thick canopy of celestial foliage. As she walked, her tightly coiled shoulders began to slacken, releasing the pent-up tension of the case's demands, if only for a short while. The ambient odors of the night filled her nostrils—a delicate blend of salty sea air intermingling with the intoxicating aroma of nearby hibiscus blooms. It was as though the island itself was administering a soothing therapy for her overstimulated senses.

Upon reaching her secluded refuge, she found her fingers fumbling slightly as they searched for the correct key. Exhaustion had lent them a clumsiness, unusual for someone whose profession required keen fine motor skills. Finally, she managed to insert the key and unlock the door, making a mental note to never underestimate the importance of physical stamina in her line of work. Despite the general safety of her location, the risk of exposing her clandestine detective activities to her family warranted stringent security measures. And so, she religiously locked her sanctuary whenever she stepped out.

Stepping into her space, she was welcomed by the warm familiarity of her own world: the worn but comforting couch that often doubled as her makeshift bed during late-night sleuthing, the desk strewn with hastily jotted notes, crime novels for inspiration, and a corkboard that served as the plotting ground for her current case's intricate web of relations and clues.

As the door closed behind her with an almost poignant click, a sense of definitive closure seemed to settle within the confined but inviting space. This was her alternate battlefield, one where mental combat against elusive adversaries took place, where the phantoms of unresolved mysteries were tackled. Tonight, however, she resolved that the battles would remain dormant, suspended in a temporal ceasefire.

Setting her alarm for four hours ahead, Sienna calculated the bare minimum rest required to prevent a plunge into the foggy abyss of deep sleep. Changing out of her day clothes and into something more conducive to relaxation, she lowered herself onto her welcoming couch, bypassing the loft bed above her, which she knew from experience could act like a comforting trap, making the act of rising all but impossible. Leaving the window ajar, the rhythmic cadence of the ocean's waves filtered in, each ebb and flow serving as a lullaby composed by nature itself.

As her eyelids grew heavy and descended like soft curtains, Sienna felt as if she were hovering in an temporary limbo, poised between the immediate, demanding realities of an intricate, multilayered investigation and the distant, hazy realm of untapped dreams and unexplored subconscious landscapes. When the dawn's early light—or more accurately, the still-dark hours just before dawn—would beckon her to wakefulness, she knew she would rise with renewed vigor and a sharpened mind. But for this brief respite, for these scant but sacred four hours, she allowed herself to be swallowed into a comforting oblivion, replenishing her spirit and girding herself for the challenges that awaited her with the new day.

23

As the soft notes of her alarm trilled through the air, Sienna's eyes fluttered open. The digital clock displayed a time most would consider unholy for waking: 3:47 AM. She sat up, stretching her arms overhead and cracking her neck side to side. The sleep had done its magic; she felt rejuvenated and keen, her mind buzzing with renewed vigor.

She silenced the alarm and swung her legs over the side of the couch, her feet meeting the cool, wooden floor. Padding over to the kitchenette, she poured herself a cup of strong, black coffee—a detective's elixir for the graveyard shift—and took a contemplative sip. Her case board caught her eye as she set her mug down, the threads of information woven across the cork surface now begging for unraveling.

Steeling herself for the day ahead, Sienna slipped back into her practical yet stylish day clothes—a simple pair of slacks and a button-up shirt that allowed ease of movement for those unpredictable chase scenes. After a quick glance at her reflection to make sure everything was in place, she gathered her bag and her ever-present notepad.

Leaving her shed, she felt a momentary pang of wistfulness for the sanctuary she was leaving behind. Yet, it quickly dissipated as her heels crunched along the gravel path, the scent of salt and foliage invigorating her senses. The night's sky was a slowly lightening tapestry of dark blue and indigo, the stars winking out one by one as dawn prepared its entrance.

Her destination was the B&B's main building, still wrapped in the deceptive tranquility of early morning. By now, the staff would be arriving for their shifts, providing her a fresh set of people to question discreetly. Time was of the essence; she needed to follow new leads before the trail went cold.

As she pushed open the main door, Sienna steeled herself for the day's interrogations. Her first target: the cleaning staff, one of whom had reported seeing Darren near the area where the locket was last seen. With her pen poised and her questions prepped, she felt a sense of exhilarating anticipation.

And so, as the first rays of the morning sun began to stretch their golden fingers over the horizon, Sienna stepped into the realm of the waking world, her heart brimming with the promise of undiscovered truths and hidden secrets.

The day was young, and she had a mystery to solve.

The moment Sienna stepped into the B&B's main building, the aroma of freshly brewed coffee mingled with the scents of baking pastries filled the air. The staff was already bustling about, the early morning hours a hive of activity to ensure everything would be ready for the guests. A polite nod here, a quick wave there—Sienna was a familiar presence, and her investigative work often kept odd hours, so nobody batted an eye at her pre-dawn arrival.

She made her way to the service area, where she knew Maria, the head of the cleaning staff, would be orchestrating the morning's chores. Maria was a no-nonsense woman in her late forties, her hair always tied back in a tight bun, giving her an air of strict efficiency. But her eyes, kind and observant, betrayed a sharp wit and a warmer nature.

"Good marnin', Maria," Sienna greeted, her voice laced with a respectful tone that always seemed to put people at ease.

"Ah, Miss Sienna, yuh up wid di birds dis mornin'. What can I do fi yuh?" Maria looked up from her clipboard, clearly curious but too polite to probe.

"I was hopin' yuh could help mi wid sump'n," Sienna began. "Ah heard dat one a yuh team saw Darren around di area where a valuable locket went missin'. Ah true?"

Maria hesitated for a moment, looking around to make sure none of her staff was within earshot. "Yes, ah did hear somethin' like dat. But yuh know how people talk, Miss Sienna. Di B&B be a hotbed fah gossip."

Sienna leaned in a little, lowering her voice. "Maria, dis be more dan just chit-chat. Ah'm investigatin' di case, an' any lead could be crucial. Can yuh let mi talk to di one who saw him?"

Maria looked into Sienna's eyes for a long, silent moment, as if weighing her sincerity. Finally, she nodded. "Alright, Miss Sienna. Yuh can speak to Lorna. But mek it quick, eh? We got a lot fi do."

"Tenki, Maria. Yuh won't regret dis," Sienna assured her before making her way to the broom closet where Lorna was pulling out cleaning supplies.

The conversation with Lorna yielded more questions than answers. She had seen Darren, yes, but it was at a time when he should have been off-duty.

And he looked flustered, almost... scared.

As Sienna thanked Lorna and left the service area, her mind was racing. The facts were stacking up, and none of them were painting a clear picture. Darren was looking more and more like a suspect, yet something told her there was more to this story than met the eye.

Her next step was clear: she had to confront Darren again, but this time, she would be armed with new information. And she couldn't shake the feeling that time was running out— both for her investigation and possibly for Darren as well.

With a renewed sense of urgency, Sienna headed toward the staff quarters. The sun was now fully awake, casting its golden light on the lush gardens and sparkling ocean beyond. But the beauty of the morning felt distant, overshadowed by the tangled web of mystery she was desperately trying to unravel.

Nicole S. Palmer

24

As Sienna navigated the dimly lit corridor and turned the corner, she was met with the beckoning light emanating from the locker room, cutting through the darkness like a beacon. A part of her hesitated, caught between the impending confrontation and the abyss of the unknown. Taking a steadying breath that seemed to fill her lungs with resolve, she stepped over the threshold and into the room. There was Darren, hunched over, his hands busy packing up his duffel bag. His shoulders looked burdened, as if weighed down by more than just physical exhaustion.

Darren's eyes lifted from the bag, making contact with Sienna's. A complex medley of emotions colored his gaze—a mixture of resignation and annoyance, tinged with a dash of vulnerability. It was as if he had anticipated this confrontation, yet hoped it would never come to pass.

"Sienna, weh yuh a do yahso?" Darren's voice carried a cautious timbre, delicately imbued with the distinct undertones of Jamaican patois, as if invoking their shared culture could serve as a buffer to the incoming storm.

"Wi need fi reason," Sienna retorted, her voice strong and confident, echoing Darren's dialect, as she locked eyes with him. The stakes were too high for pleasantries or hesitations. This was a conversation that could no longer be deferred.

A heavy moment passed between them, the air pregnant with anticipation, before Darren finally put his bag down. "Alright, but mek it quick," he said, seemingly preparing himself for what might come next, as if bracing for an impact.

Opting for directness over subtlety, Sienna cut straight to the heart of the matter. "Mi chat to Lorna dis mawnin'. She tell mi seh she see yuh near weh di locket missin', a time when yuh suppos' to off duty. How yuh explain dat?" Her words hung in the air like a looming thundercloud, charged with a tension begging for release.

For an instant, Darren's eyes widened in a momentary flash of vulnerability. It was as if he were a deer caught in the unforgiving headlights of revelation. But then, he did something that Sienna hadn't anticipated at all. His hands reached out to grip hers with a firm intensity, his eyes locking onto hers, burning with a cocktail of emotions: fear, urgency, and something that resembled regret.

"Stop dig up, Sienna. Fi yuh own good. Mi mek a mistake fi involve yuh," Darren's voice carried a heightened sense of trepidation. It was as though he was pleading with her, begging her to retreat from the precipice on which they both now stood.

This abrupt gesture and the genuine fear in Darren's voice startled Sienna. The atmosphere felt charged, like a room filled with gas fumes, one spark away from ignition. She had never seen this side of Darren. He looked vulnerable, his eyes almost glistening as if on the cusp of tears.

"Darren, wa really a gwaan? How yuh wrap up inna dis?" Her words came out as a near whisper, tinged with a tremor that betrayed her own escalating fear.

Darren didn't answer. As if jolted by a sudden realization, he released her hands with a surprising swiftness, grabbed his bag with a newfound urgency and stood up. "Mi sorry," he mumbled, his voice strained to the point of breaking. And with that, he made a hasty exit.

Just as he was about to vanish into the shadows of the corridor, a crumpled piece of paper slipped out of his pocket, fluttering to the ground like a fallen leaf. Before Sienna could shout to call him back, the locker room door slammed shut with a jarring finality, encapsulating her in a room now awash with metaphorical darkness and a cacophony of unanswered questions.

With her heart hammering in her chest, as if echoing the frenzied beat of a jungle drum, Sienna stooped down to retrieve the crumpled paper. Her fingers trembling, she unfolded it carefully, revealing its contents. She instantly recognized the stationery; it was eerily identical to the notes she had discovered in his locker earlier in the week. Her eyes grew wider, if that were possible, as she read the ominous message, scrawled in a harried hand with red ink: "GIVE ME BACK THE LOCKET OR IT WILL BE THE END OF YOU."

A shiver coursed through her, electrifying her from head to toe. The note was a harbinger of things much darker and more dangerous than she had ever anticipated. She was confronted with a stark revelation: Darren was ensnared in a web far more complex and perilous than she had ever imagined. And by the inexorable logic of her involvement, she was now entangled in it as well, standing on the edge of a vortex that threatened to pull them both into its ominous depths.

Nicole S. Palmer

25

The weight of what she had discovered about Darren gnawed at Sienna as she sat in the dim light of her shed, her eyes flitting back and forth between the corkboard of clues and the pictures of handwritten threats. She had initially believed Darren about the locket being a keepsake from his grandmother. But if the note in Darren's locker had revealed anything, it was that the locket was something worth threatening a life over. And more perplexingly, Darren had lied about its origins. So, whose locket was it? And why had he lied?

Darren's rapidly complicating role in this affair began to appear less like an anchor and more like a weight pulling her down into uncharted, and perhaps, treacherous waters. With Darren's lie now mingling with the already complex web of clues and half-truths, Sienna felt a new urgency. Someone was issuing threats over this locket. Someone wanted it badly enough to terrorize Darren, and possibly, harm her.

In a case shrouded in lies and threats, time was the one thing she couldn't afford to lose. She looked at her clock; it read 5:00 AM. Sleep was out of the question. DShe stepped outside her shed, taking a seat on her cherished rocking chair that overlooked the ocean. The rhythmic ebb and flow of the waves comforted her, as they always did. This was her sanctuary, her sacred space for focus and clarity. The rolling tides seemed to echo her own oscillating thoughts—now at a peak of clarity, then receding into the mists of uncertainty.

As she rocked gently, absorbing the predawn serenity, her thoughts circled back to her plan to visit Sheryl later. Sheryl was well-connected, a human repository of the island's rumors and secrets. But Sienna now realized that she'd need to be cautious, as divulging too much could put her informant in danger as well. This case was no longer a simple matter of curiosity; real lives were now at stake, including her own.

The first hint of dawn began to lighten the horizon, painting the sky with shades of pink and orange. As the new day broke, Sienna knew she had to return to her other world, the one where she was merely the helpful daughter at her family's B&B, not a budding detective entangled in a web of deceit and danger. She rose from her chair, took a deep breath to absorb one last gulp of salty air, and made her way back to the B&B.

Puppa was already in the kitchen when she arrived, his eyes slightly surprised but happy to see her so early. "Gud mornin', Sienna," he greeted, his tone infused with both curiosity and a hint of concern, as if wondering what brought her into the kitchen at such an early hour.

"Mornin', Puppa," she replied with an affectionate smile, picking up a stack of pans. "Mi thought yuh could use a licked help prepping fi di day."

As she went about helping Puppa, Sienna felt the double life she was leading pull at her from both sides. On the one hand, the comforting normality of family and routine; on the other, the dark, unfolding mystery that seemed to grow more tangled with each passing day. It was a delicate balance, a tightrope she walked with practiced care. Yet even as she measured out ingredients for the morning's breakfast, her mind was on another kind of measurement altogether—one involving the delicate calibration of truth and deception, risk and reward.

The morning sun streamed through the windows, flooding the B&B's cozy kitchen with light. Yet Sienna felt a shadow pass over her. The events of last night, Darren's lies, the threats— all loomed large in her mind. But for now, in this sunlit kitchen, she could pretend to be just Sienna, the diligent daughter, the loving family member, leaving the role of Sienna, the detective, waiting in the wings. It was a performance, a charade, and the stakes were life and death.

So she smiled at Puppa, chatted about the weather, and focused on the culinary tasks at hand. But inside, she was piecing together a puzzle, one that had the potential to shatter the peaceful world she loved so dearly. And as she balanced both worlds, one of comforting familial normality and one of dangerous intrigue, Sienna knew that sooner or later, something would have to give. The question was, what would it be? And was she ready to face the consequences?

26

As the breakfast rush wound down at the B&B, Sienna began to feel the weight of her double life becoming increasingly hard to bear. On the surface, everything appeared idyllic; guests were chatting happily, the smell of freshly cooked bacon and eggs lingered in the air, and Puppa was in his usual good spirits, cracking jokes with the visitors. But Sienna knew better. With each passing minute, the unresolved case hung over her like a dark cloud, its shadow growing larger and more ominous.

Finally, finding a break in her chores, Sienna slips away under the pretense of running an errand for the B&B. Her real destination was Sheryl's quaint little shop down by the marina. The shop was a hodgepodge of knick-knacks, island souvenirs, and essential supplies for both locals and tourists. But Sienna wasn't there to shop; she was there to gather information.

When she enters, Sheryl greets her warmly, "Sienna, mi gyal! How yuh deh?"

"Gud, mi gud. Yuh know how di ting set," Sienna replies, feigning casualness.

Sheryl senses the tension, her eyes narrowing ever so slightly, "So wah bring yuh down mi side today?"

"A jus a lickle matter mi wudda like yuh insight pon," Sienna says cautiously.

Sheryl leans in, intrigued, "Talk to mi, yuh know mi ears always open."

Sienna, aware that Sheryl is an asset in her investigative pursuits, is deliberately vague. "Yuh hear anyting bout a locket dis pas days? Anyting at all?"

For a moment, Sheryl's eyes glint with a combination of understanding and perhaps a dash of excitement. "Well, now dat yuh mention it, sumtin interesting did come up."

Sienna leans in closer. She needs this lead.

Sheryl describes a wealthy couple she noticed at a recent island party. "Di man an di woman dem dressed like dem just walk outta a magazine, yuh nuh. Im inna a tailored suit, an she in one of dem long gowns, di sort yuh see pon red carpet."

Sienna felt her impatience rising; she had no time for fashion commentary. But just as she's about to interrupt, Sheryl gives her a knowing smile and continues.

"But yuh know wah di funniest ting? Di woman a wear one small, gold locket roun' her neck. Look like sump'n yuh woulda find inna bargain bin. Stick out like a sore thumb, mi tell yuh."

Sienna's eyes widen, and her ears feel as if they've just perked up. "Tell mi again, Sheryl."

Sheryl, looking quite pleased with herself, repeats, "Mi seh di woman did a wear di locket 'round her neck, an mi nuh mistake 'bout it."

Sienna's mind is spinning. The locket that she's been chasing, the one wrapped up in lies, threats, and now possibly even a dangerous family secret, had been hanging openly around some woman's neck at a party. Could it be the same locket?

Feeling both overwhelmed and invigorated by this new piece of the puzzle, Sienna thanks Sheryl for her invaluable insight. "Nuff respect, Sheryl. Yuh nuh know how much dis help mi."

Sienna strides out of Sheryl's shop, her mind awash with conflicting emotions and revelations. The small, heart-shaped locket—its intricate yet unassuming design belying its contentious history—had appeared at a party, around the neck of a lavishly dressed woman. The very locket that

Darren had spun lies around, the one entangled in a web of threats against him, was now more important than ever.

The stakes have been raised, and Sienna finds herself at a crucial crossroads. The threat looms closer, yet the pull of the mystery is too strong to resist. Should she protect herself and her family by walking away, or should she dive even deeper, risking it all for the sake of the truth?

As Sienna contemplated her next move, she recalled the crumpled note that had flown out of Darren's pocket, the inked warning in red capital letters: "GIVE ME BACK THE LOCKET OR IT WILL BE THE END OF YOU." The veiled threat was against Darren, not her, but she felt increasingly drawn into the perilous whirlpool surrounding the locket.

Sienna's phone buzzes in her pocket. It's a message from Darren. She unlocks her phone, and her eyes scan the few words on the screen: "We need to talk. Urgent."

No direct threat, but the urgency in Darren's text still sends a shiver down her spine. The stakes are higher than she'd ever anticipated. She needs to speak with Darren, but a nagging caution reminds her that delving deeper might pull her further into the very threats that haunt him. Darren's warnings to stay away freshly echoed in her mind, and she grappled with the delicate balance of her two lives. One as a dutiful daughter, helping run the family's B&B, and another as a relentless seeker of truth who won't rest until this puzzling case was solved.

Back at the B&B, her family was absorbed in their daily tasks, blissfully unaware of Sienna's inner turmoil. Her Auntie Faye was checking guest reservations on the computer, Mumma was instructing a staff member on room preparations, and her siblings are absorbed in their own worlds. For Sienna, the B&B isn't just a home or a business; it's a façade behind which she conducts her investigations, her own personal theater of duality.

She feels the weight of her next decision. Should she heed Darren's veiled warnings and pull back, or should she confront him and risk delving deeper into this intricate and dangerous puzzle? Time is of the essence, but the decision she's about to make is not to be taken lightly. This is no mere dalliance in detective work; it's a dangerous game now. And as she hurriedly makes her way back to the B&B, a million and one thoughts flooding her psyche, Sienna knows that her next move could change everything.

27

Sienna quickens her pace, her sandals crunching over the path of crushed seashells that leads to the B&B's main entrance. The foliage on either side is lush, a verdant frame of palm fronds, blooming hibiscus, and ferns that seem to whisper secrets to one another. But the tropical serenity does little to calm the churn of anxiety inside her. Puppa stands like a sentinel at the doorway, his arms crossed over his barrel chest, his eyes narrow and watchful as they settle on her.

Sienna's heart leaps into her throat and then seems to plummet into her stomach. Gone are her illusions of sliding back into the kitchen unnoticed. Puppa's posture alone tells her that much.

"Wat tek yuh suh long, Sienna? Yuh seh yuh did ah run quick errand, but yuh tek longa dan mi expect," his voice underlain by a thread of concern that belies his stern expression.

Sienna pauses for a beat, her eyes meeting Puppa's. She can see a lifetime of wisdom reflected there, alongside something else—was it suspicion? "Mi run into some traffic, Puppa, plus di errand tek a likkle more time than mi thought."

Puppa studies her, his gaze penetrating. She feels like an open book under his scrutiny, her secrets inked on her face in a language he can easily read. Finally, his arms uncross, but his eyes never leave her face.

"Careful how yuh walk, Sienna," his voice tinged with a caution that sends a frisson of unease down Sienna's spine.

"Mi know, Puppa, mi know. Mi ah be careful, mi promise," she replies, swallowing hard. Her voice carries a gravity that matches his own. She senses the weight of the unspoken words that hang in the air between them—words of mysteries unraveling, of lives in the balance, and of trust under the threat of erosion.

Puppa nods slowly, but his expression tells Sienna he only half believes her excuse or that she'll heed his advice to be careful.

"Well, we av a full house today, and di food nah mek itself."

"Mi deh deh inna few, Puppa," she replies, grateful for the opportunity to submerge herself in something other than her spiraling thoughts.

"Mek haste. Mi wan yuh inna di kitchen in less than a few, yuh ere?" The sternness in his voice is unmistakable. Puppa lets out a deep sigh, shakes his head and walks off. Sienna holds back the all-too-familiar tears of disappointing her Puppa yet again. She questioned whether the price she was paying for her double life was too high. Taking a moment to push those thoughts aside, she gathered her composure and headed to the kitchen to help.

Once inside the fragrant kitchen, surrounded by the comforting chaos of sizzling pans and clinking utensils, Sienna slips into a routine that's as familiar as it is grounding. The aroma of ackee and saltfish melds with the scent of freshly brewed Blue Mountain coffee, filling the air and momentarily pushing aside her concerns.

But then her phone buzzes, drawing her out of the culinary ballet she and her father perform each morning. It's a text from Darren: "Meet mi at di cliff overlookin' East Bay. Noon."

The message sends a jolt through her. The cliff is remote, far from prying eyes and well-meaning neighbors. Darren's choice of meeting place tells her that what he has to say is serious, perhaps dangerous.

"Everyting gud?" Puppa asks, his eyes narrowing as he senses her distraction.

"Yeah, Puppa, all is ok," she assures him, forcing a smile. "A jus a friend wah fi meet up layta."

"Hmm," he grunts softly, not entirely convinced but choosing to let it go. "Alright, but memba we haffi prep fi lunch service, so nuh get ketch up inna no long meetin', zeen?"

"Yes, Puppa," she promises, even as her mind races with questions and scenarios, each more confounding than the last.

As Sienna continues to slice, mix, and fry, her actions become almost automatic, freeing her mind to ponder the enigma that has enveloped her life. The locket, the threats against Darren, and now a mysterious meeting at an isolated cliff—all these fragments refuse to coalesce into a picture she can understand. But regardless of the danger or the questions that remain, Sienna knows she'll go to that cliff. Because whatever puzzle Darren is a part of, she's committed to solving it.

28

As Sienna navigated the maze of hallways and charmingly eclectic rooms that made up the Bailey family's Bed & Breakfast, she couldn't shake the nervous tremor in her hands. Her thoughts were like an ever-tightening knot, each loop representing a question she had for Darren. Was he lying? Was he in danger? Was he the danger? She was almost at the front door, her hand hovering over the knob, about to step into the sunny embrace of the morning, when a soothing voice wafted through the air and brought her to a standstill.

"Sienna, whey yuh ah go in such a hurry, mi child?" The voice was unmistakable: Grace Bailey, better known as Mumma. Sienna was so focused on getting to the bottom of the web she found herself in, she didn't notice that Mumma had followed her out of the kitchen. She wore a floral apron that had seen better days, and a dishtowel was casually slung over her shoulder. Her dark eyes squinting slightly as she studied her daughter. The corners of her mouth curved into a gentle smile, but there was an undercurrent of maternal concern in her eyes.

Caught off guard, Sienna hesitated, choosing her words carefully. "Ah jus' have sump'n mi need fi sort out, Mumma. Nuttin' to worry about."

Mumma walked closer, wiping her hands on her apron. "Yuh sure everything alright? Yuh face look like yuh carry di whole world pon yuh shoulda. An' don't tell mi it's nuttin', 'cause mi cyan see it's sump'n."

Sienna sighed deeply, her shoulders dropping as if conceding to the invisible weight they carried. She looked into Mumma's eyes, wells of wisdom and understanding, and felt a tug at her heartstrings. "Ah just confused, Mumma. Mi feel like mi inna di middle of a storm an' mi cyaan find mi way out."

Mumma nodded, her expression was a combination of empathy, concern, and love. "Life is full a starms, Sienna, but rememba yuh don't haffi go thru dem alone. Mi an' yuh Puppa, wi always ere fi yuh."

Sienna looked at her Mumma and felt a sense of comfort wash over her, tempering the whirlpool of anxiety that churned within. "Ah know dat, Mumma. An' it means di world to mi. Mi just need fi figure out some tings on mi own, first. You know, serious tings."

With a knowing look and doing her best to suppress a smile at Sienna's characterization of the seriousness of things, Mumma took a step closer and opened her arms wide. Sienna walked into her embrace, feeling a flood of warmth envelop her, as if she had momentarily stepped back into the simpler times of her childhood. "Grown up business is hard, mi child. But rememba, yuh can always talk to mi. We ah family, an' family stick togedda."

Emotion swelled in Sienna's chest, and she clung to her mother for a moment longer. "Thank yuh, Mumma. Mi promise mi will talk to yuh when mi figure out how to put mi thoughts into words. Fi now, mi need fi clear mi head an' mek some decisions."

Mumma released her, placing a gentle hand on Sienna's cheek before giving her a tender kiss on the forehead. "Gwan then, sort out wha yuh need fi sort out. But no stray too far or too lang. Yuh know how yuh Puppa get wen im start fi worry."

Sienna chuckled softly, imagining her father's more authoritarian, 'bad cop' approach to parenting. "Mi know, Mumma, no worries. Mi will be careful. Mi soon come back."

Her mother's eyes twinkled one last time before she turned back toward the kitchen, "Ah holding yuh to dat, yuh hear?"

With her mother's words of wisdom echoing like a comforting melody in her ears, Sienna finally stepped out of the B&B. Though she was still embroiled in uncertainty and complex feelings, the encounter with Mumma had gifted her a momentary reprieve. As she walked away, her stride regained a bit of its usual confidence. With her family's love as her bedrock and her mother's counsel as her guide, Sienna felt fortified to face whatever lay ahead, including her pending conversation with Darren. It was as if a layer of fog had lifted, allowing her a moment of clarity and resolve in a life that had recently become anything but clear.

29

For many tourists, navigating the intricate footpaths to the overlook at East Bay could be a disorienting experience. The trails were like serpentine vines, winding through a dense thicket of foliage, taking sudden, unpredictable turns that seemed designed to confound. But Sienna, with her islander's intuition and intimate knowledge of the terrain, could traverse these paths with her eyes closed. Raised on the island's natural beauty and mysteries, she understood the nuances of each twist and turn as intimately as she knew the lines that crisscrossed her palm.

The earth beneath her feet seemed to pulse with a rich, damp aroma, a smell that blended seamlessly with the salty tang carried in from the sea. This combination of scents was hypnotic in its simplicity, lulling her into a state of alert serenity. As she advanced along the trail, her feet moved in a rhythmic dance with the earth, instinctively dodging the roots that protruded like gnarled fingers, avoiding the stones strewn haphazardly, as if flung by some capricious giant.

At one stretch, the path contracted sharply, sandwiched between a pair of ancient boulders, their surfaces velvety with the green embrace of moss. The space was narrow, offering just enough room for a single body to slide through. To the uninitiated, it might have appeared daunting or inscrutable. But for Sienna, it was merely another characteristic landmark, and she glided through it as effortlessly as water flowing down a stream.

As she meandered along, fingers of sunlight reached down through the breaks in the leafy canopy overhead, creating patches of dappled light and shadow that played on the forest floor. The undergrowth was punctuated by occasional bursts of color from flowering plants. Here, a red hibiscus with its open, trumpet-like bloom; there, golden bells of allamanda hung like celestial ornaments; elsewhere, clusters of morning glories unfurled their purplish-blue trumpets to welcome the day. This kaleidoscopic display added a layer of visual richness to Sienna's journey.

As she moved closer to her destination, the pulse of the ocean became more pronounced, its sound weaving through the other natural melodies to create a symphony that seemed to reverberate with her own heartbeat. The call of the sea drew her like a siren's song, urging her to quicken her pace.

At last, she emerged from the cocoon of the forest and stepped onto the precipice of the cliff. What lay before her was a sight that no matter how many times she'd seen it, never failed to steal her breath away. The jagged rocks below looked like the fossilized teeth of some mythical sea beast, gnashing at the sky. They framed an expansive view of the ocean, an undulating canvas awash in varying shades of blue, from the pale aquamarines near the shore to the deep, impenetrable sapphires that marked unfathomable depths.

The cliff was a living museum of geological time, its facade layered with strata that spoke of epochs long past. The relentless grind of wind, water, and time had etched ornate patterns into the stone, turning it into a monumental sculpture crafted by nature's own hand. Sienna had a favored spot on this cliff—a somewhat flat boulder set a respectful distance from the very edge. It offered the double allure of a staggering view and a reassuring sense of safety.

She sat down and for a moment lost herself in the ceaseless motion of the sea below. This place had always served as her sanctuary, a refuge from the world where her thoughts could roam free, uncluttered by the mundane distractions that life incessantly offered. Now, more than ever, she needed to find clarity amid the chaos that had invaded her life.

30

Sienna's eyes narrowed, her fingers drumming on her knee. The cliff's majestic view felt like a mocking backdrop to the gnawing anxiety that was now twisting inside her. Darren had always been punctual, especially for matters as grave as the one they were embroiled in. His absence didn't just feel odd; it felt alarming.

Minutes stretched into what felt like small eternities. With each passing moment, the sense of foreboding intensified, curling in her stomach like a dark fog. Sienna finally stood up, scanning the area meticulously, her detective instincts now fully activated. She looked beyond the usual spots— behind a protruding rock formation, around the bend that led to a hidden nook favored by couples seeking solitude. Nothing.

Her eyes finally settled on something that didn't belong in this natural tableau: a small but unmistakable puddle of blood, its color a dark, jarring contrast against the rocky cliffside. Her heart plummeted into her stomach. Something terrible had happened here. As if to punctuate the thought, a soft, anguished moan floated up from below.

Sienna rushed to the edge and peered down cautiously. There, on a jagged outcrop some distance below, was Darren. He was sprawled out, his body contorted in a manner that screamed of injury and pain. His face was flushed, eyes scrunched in agony, and a dark patch of blood had stained his shirt. That he had not tumbled all the way down to the ocean was a small miracle, but his situation was perilous nonetheless.

Her mind raced through options. To descend the craggy cliffside was dangerous, even for an islander familiar with its treacherous quirks. But time was of the essence, and Darren was clearly in dire straits. Taking a deep, steadying breath, she began her descent. Each step was calculated, each grip verified twice before shifting her weight. A single misstep could lead to disaster for both of them.

Sienna's experience navigating the island's rocky terrain paid off. Within minutes that felt like hours, she reached Darren. Up close, his condition was worse than she had initially thought. His face was ashen except for the streaks of dirt and dried blood, and his eyes fluttered open weakly as she reached him.

"Darren, what happened?" Sienna's voice was a mix of relief and urgent concern.

He moaned, grimacing as he tried to adjust his position. "Sienna... ah, jah know... I mess up. Mi shouldn't drag yuh into dis."

His words slurred and carried a tremor that was palpable. She needed to get Darren help, but the mystery of what had transpired—and what it meant for both of them—loomed larger than ever.

Sienna's gaze was like flint as she leaned closer, her fingers carefully avoiding Darren's visible injuries. The view behind her had long ceased to register as scenic. The beauty of the cliffs, the majesty of the ocean—none of it mattered. The palette of natural colors had been replaced by the monochromatic urgency of the situation: Darren, injured and possibly in danger, both of them tangled in a web that neither fully understood.

"Talk to mi, Darren. Ah need yuh to be clear. What mess yuh talkin' about? What yuh drag mi into?" The words tumbled out in a rush, fueled by a desperation she couldn't mask.

Darren coughed painfully, his eyes searching hers, clouded by a mix of regret and confusion. "Ah... ah neva thought dem woulda go so fa. Mi innocent plan backfire, Sienna. Mi never mean fi get yuh involved, but dem people, dem ah not playin' around."

Sienna felt a shiver snake down her spine, her eyes widening. "People? What people, Darren? Yuh ah talk in riddles and mi ah nuh got di time. Di wealthy couple at di big bash."

Darren's eyes widened with surprise at Sienna's last question. He winced, clearly struggling to find the right words or perhaps grappling with the decision to divulge them. "Mi sorry. Mi didn't mean fi lie to yuh. Mi beg yuh please forgive mi." Darren uttered the words in between short, labored breaths, as tears rolled down his bruised and battered face.

"Shhhh, shhhh. Nuh worry yuhself now, Darren. Nuh worry yuhself." Sienna's voice quivered as she held back tears of her own. As much as she wanted to know more, she had to focus on keeping Darren as stable as possible until help could arrive.

Darren looked up, his eyes dark pools of sorrow. "Mi wanted to protect yuh. But it look like mi just put yuh inna more danger."

Sienna shook her head, battling a surge of emotions. Anger, betrayal, but also an overwhelming concern for Darren's immediate safety clouded her thoughts. "We need fi focus, Darren. Mi go deal wid yuh foolishness later," she said, half-jokingly in hopes of eliciting a smile. "First, mi need fi get yuh off dis cliff."

He nodded, gritting his teeth as she assessed his injuries, contemplating the best way to move him—if she could at all. "Sienna, if anyting happen to mi—"

Her eyes widened again, this time accompanied by a knot tightening in her stomach. "Mi hope it nuh come to dat, Darren. But promise mi, yuh go explain everyting if we get outta dis."

Darren managed a weak smile. "Promise, Sienna. If mi make it outta dis, mi go spill everyting."

She looked at Darren once more and gently lifted his shirt. His stomach was badly bruised and discolored. The bruising appeared to spread before her eyes. She did her best to contain the fear threatening to overwhelm her. These were telltale signs of internal bleeding. She had no way of knowing what other more critical injuries Darren had suffered at the hands of the unknown assailants. She couldn't risk moving him, as it could make his situation even worse.

31

Sienna's hands shook as she fished her phone from her back pocket, dialing the emergency number with frantic fingers. "Mi deh pon di cliffside, an' sump'n bad happen to mi fren Darren. Him injured bad, yuh understan'? Wi need help!"

After explaining their precarious location, the operator confirmed what Sienna had feared: no ambulance could navigate the difficult terrain to reach them. The air chopper was dispatched instead. A nerve-wracking span of minutes passed, filled only by the sound of Darren's labored breathing and the distant whir of helicopter blades growing steadily louder.

Finally, the chopper appeared above them, a roaring behemoth against the blue sky. The strong downdraft of its blades sent loose pebbles and dirt scattering. Two paramedics rappelled down, quickly assessing Darren's condition before strapping him into a stretcher and winching both him and Sienna up to the aircraft. They were airlifted to the local hospital, where Darren was immediately rushed into the operating room.

As Sienna sat in the sterile hospital waiting area, she felt a shiver run down her spine. The clock on the wall ticked loudly, each second stretching into eternity. She was startled by the sudden influx of people bursting through the hospital doors. It was her family and the B&B staff, their faces etched with concern and disbelief.

Seeing her parents, Sienna's eyes met theirs. Their gaze was not one of inquiry or reprimand, but one filled with love and a profound sense of relief that their daughter was unharmed. Both stretched out their hands toward her. She couldn't help but crumble, tears cascading down her face as she fell into their embrace. No words were needed. Now was not a time for questions, for accusations, or for piecing together the fragmented mystery that had led to this moment. Now was a time for comfort, for family, and for the unspoken but deeply felt reassurance that, in the midst of chaos and unanswered questions, they would face whatever came next as one.

Just as Sienna felt the warmth of her parents' embrace start to ease the day's tension, an all-too-familiar voice pierced the air, simultaneously grating and comforting in its familiarity.

"Sienna, yuh really tek di cake, yuh know. Wha yuh a do up dere on di cliff, eh? Yuh coulda dead!"

It was Marley, her older sister, leaning against the entrance of the waiting room, arms folded and eyes a mix of annoyance and concern. She had always been the pragmatic one, the sister who equated worry with stern words and head-shaking.

Sienna sighed, extracting herself from her parents' arms to face her sister. "Marley, now nuh di time fi dat. It serious, sump'n really bad happen to Darren."

"Ah know it serious, mi nuh blind! But dat nuh mean yuh fi put yuhself inna danger," Marley retorted, stepping closer. Her eyes were narrowed but glinted with the kind of love that only shows itself through protective vexation. "Yuh tink she Mumma and Puppa need fi worry 'bout yuh pon top a everyting else?"

Sienna opened her mouth to reply but was interrupted by a small but powerful force that wedged itself between the two sisters, effectively halting their exchange. It was Lily, the youngest of the three. With an arm around each of her sisters, she looked up at them, her eyes bright and earnest.

"Lil, wha yuh a do?" Marley grumbled, clearly not thrilled at the intrusion.

Ignoring Marley's protest, Lily hugged them both tightly. Leaning into Sienna, she whispered, "Wha Marley try fi say is dat she glad yuh okay, ah nuh tru, Marley?"

Marley rolled her eyes but then begrudgingly grunted, "Yeah, mi glad yuh okay, but yuh still gonna hear from mi, yuh get mi?"

Sienna chuckled softly, grateful for her sisters despite their complexities. For a moment, they all squeezed each other tightly, forming a trio bound not just by blood, but by the multitude of unspoken emotions that swirled around them—fear, relief, love, and the commitment to face whatever life had in store head on.

The Lost Locket

32

After what seemed like an eternity, a doctor emerged from the operating room, his face wearing a mixture of exhaustion and relief. "Im stabilize now," he began, locking eyes with Sienna and her family. "Im lose nuff blood an' av some broken ribs, but im shoulda recover ova time. Family only cyan see him."

Sienna felt a pang of disappointment; she was not family, yet she felt a familial connection, complicated as it was by recent events. Her parents, sensing her struggle, spoke up. "Dactah, a Sienna find im an' bring im yah so. She a close like family. She cyan go in?"

After a moment's hesitation, the doctor nodded. "Alright, but mek it quick. Im need fi rest up."

Sienna walked into the dimly lit room, her heart pounding as she saw Darren's bruised and battered face. His eyes fluttered open, and for a moment, they locked gazes. A thousand unspoken questions hovered in the air between them.

Darren's eyes met Sienna's as he began to speak. "Listen, mi haffi tell yuh everyting now," he said weakly. "Di locket... it nuh belong to mi or mi granny. Ah did tek it from some fancy British couple dat was rude an' mean to di staff."

Sienna's eyes widened, but she stayed silent, urging him to continue.

"Mi find di locket 'pon di ground afta dem lef di dining room. Mi tink di clasp mussi bruk. Mi did tek it an' hide it in one unoccupied room, mi plan was to gi it back lata an' play di hero, maybe get a nice tip."

Sienna felt a mix of mild relief and mdisappointment. Relief that the locket was seemingly not tied to anything more sinister, but disappointment in Darren for lying.

"Mi go back to di room fi get di locket, but it gone, jus' like dat. So when di woman come back a look fah it, mi decide mi aguh seh mi put it inna di lost an' found, but now it nuh deh deh. Dem neva believe mi, an' dem say mi responsible fah it. Dat's how di threatening message dem start."

Darren's eyes were filled with regret. "Sienna, mi neva expect it would come to dis. Ah jus' wanted to... Ah nuh know... teach dem a lesson?"

Sienna felt a torrent of emotions but understood this was not the time for recriminations. "Darren, dis ting put yuh life inna danger. Dis locket must haffi have some kinda value we nuh know 'bout."

Darren nodded, his eyes meeting hers one last time before he closed them. "Sienna, be careful. Dis nuh simple as it look."

As Sienna left the room, she was more determined than ever. The looming questions around the locket and the peril it had brought upon Darren made her investigation not just a quest for truth but a matter of life and death. She returned to the waiting room where her family had congregated, each wrapped up in their own thoughts and concerns.

Puppa, approached her, squeezing her hand gently. "Yuh look like yuh have whole heap 'pon yuh mind, Sienna. Wah yuh a plan fi do now?"

Sienna met his gaze, her eyes filled with a resolve that surprised even her. "Mi haffi end dis, Puppa. Mi haffi find out wah really a gwaan an' mek it right."

Puppa nodded solemnly, his eyes filled with a mixture of pride and fear. She expected more resistance from him, of all people. Yet all he said was, "Jus' memba, yuh nuh alone. Wi deh yah, all ah wi."

Sienna felt a newfound sense of purpose fill her. The road ahead was uncertain and fraught with peril, but she was not walking it alone. And that gave her the strength to face whatever lay ahead.

Sienna's determination was cemented now. As her family continued their anxious vigil in the waiting room, she felt her phone buzz. It was a message from Sheryl. "Sienna, sump'n new come up 'bout di locket. Ah think yuh need fi hear dis."

Sienna felt a complex swirl of emotions as she read Sheryl's urgent message. She glanced at her family, their faces etched with concern but also hope, brought on by Darren's stabilized condition. "Puppa, Mumma, mi need fi step out fi a likkle bit. A lead come in, mi feel it crucial."

Mumma locked eyes with her, "Yuh sure yuh need fi go now? Darren jus' stabilize."

Sienna pulled her into a hug, "Mumma, mi know. But ah feel dis might be di way to mek tings right, to put an end to all a dis."

Puppa broke in, "Sienna, yuh know seh ah dangerous situation dis. Take Terrence wid yuh."

The suggestion made her skin bristle— Terrence was great but sometimes overprotective. However, she caught the worried glint in her parents' eyes and realized this wasn't the time to argue. "Alright, mi will."

Terrence almost leapt from his seat, his face plastered with a wide grin that was all too smug. Sienna resisted the overwhelming urge to roll her eyes at him in disgust. "Mi will tek gud care of her, nuh worry yuhself. She inna gud hands," he said reassuringly to Mumma and Puppa.

Sienna held her tongue from making a disparaging and cutting remark, and forced a smile. "Mek haste, Terrence! Wi haffi gwan!" Sienna shouted back the command as she headed out the doors of the hospital. Terrence had to run to catch up. As she walked to Terrence's car, he managed to sprint ahead of her and open the passenger door. Now out of the vigilant eyes of her family, Sienna gave him the most exaggerated of eye rolls as she shook her head. Terrence simply flashed a smile and made a dramatic bow as he gestured toward the seat.

All Sienna could do was very pointedly kiss her teeth at him while she reluctantly plopped herself into his car. As they began to head out, Terrence opened his mouth to make a clever comment, but was met by Sienna's icy stare, daring him to do anything other than drive her to Shery's. He was well acquainted with what came next and knew none who'd survived the tongue lashing that followed. So he closed his mouth, turned to face the road and they drove in silence.

33

As Sienna and Terrence pushed through the beaded curtain into Sheryl's dimly lit shop, the air felt thick and heavy, as if soaked with tension. Sheryl's hands trembled slightly as she shuffled some items on her counter. Beads of sweat glistened on her forehead, and her eyes were wide, almost frantic. "Sienna, mi so glad yuh could come so quick. Mi got sump'n crucial fi tell yuh, sump'n weh mi think a tie up to everyting weh a happen."

Sienna leaned in closer, her eyes locked onto Sheryl's as if trying to gauge the depth of her sincerity. "Alright, Sheryl. Chat to mi. Wha exactly yuh see?"

Gathering herself, Sheryl's voice quivered with urgency. "Mi see di woman and di man again, yuh know, di one wid di mysterious locket. Dem was inna corner of a café down di road, talkin' like dem inna some kinda spy movie or sump'n. Di woman a mention a 'recovery operation,' an' mi hear ar say clear as day dat dem haffi get di locket back before dem leave di island tomorrow marnin'."

Sienna's heart pounded in her chest; her pulse quickened with every beat. "Hold on, Sheryl. Yuh a tell mi dem a plan fi leave tomorrow marnin'? Yuh sure yuh nuh mishear?"

"Mi sure as sugar, Sienna," Sheryl emphatically responded, her face a combination of fear and satisfaction. "Mi nuh want fi eavesdrop, but di ting sound serious. Mi coulda feel di weight of ar words."

Terrence, who'd been lingering silently near the mystical display of crystals at the doorway, now stepped forward. "Mi been listenin' to di whole ting. Sienna, how yuh think we should proceed? It seem like time a run out pon we."

Sienna glanced at Terrence, her eyes narrowing momentarily. At this point, she had no option but to accept him as an unexpected ally, albeit one she never asked for. "Terrence, mi feel di urgency deep inna mi bones. We cyaan sit back an' watch dis unfold. Mi feel like wi need fi tek control of di narrative."

Terrence's eyes brightened, a glint of understanding and perhaps even admiration in them. "Ah, so what's di very first move, then? Wi headin' straight back to di B&B to dig up sump'n?"

Sienna took a deep breath, wrestling with her thoughts for a moment before answering. "Yes, mi think so. If dis woman so desperate to get dis locket, den dere mus be clues back at di B&B. Mi feel like if we shake di tree hard enough, sump'n a go fall out. We haffi uncover how dis couple, di locket, an' all dis madness intertwine."

Sheryl's expression shifted to one of genuine concern mixed with reluctant approval. "Sienna, mi haffi ask yuh... yuh sure yuh up fi all dis? Dis ting sound more an' more dangerous by di minute."

Sienna tightened her lips, her eyes full of fierce resolve. "Sheryl, mi don't really have a choice inna dis. Mi cyaan allow dese people an' whoever dem work fa fi get away, especially afta wha dem do to Darren. It nah go suh."

Feeling a swirling blend of dread and resolve envelop her, Sienna turned sharply on her heels and made her way out of the dim shop. Terrence fell in step behind her, his face etched with a seriousness that matched hers. The next day was clearly setting up to be pivotal—a day of reckoning not just for her and Darren, but for everyone entangled in this increasingly dangerous affair over a seemingly innocuous locket. It was as if the universe itself was holding its breath, waiting for her to take the reins. She was done being a bystander in her own life story; it was high time she became its author.

34

The ride back to the B&B was filled with a silence so tense it was visible and palpable. Terrence knew better than to interrupt Sienna when that intense, faraway look was etched across her face. So he played the role of dutiful driver and allowed her time in her thoughts. The time seemed to fly by and crawl all at once on the drive back. As Terrence pulled up to the entrance.

Feeling a mixture of urgency and hope, Sienna nodded to Terrence as she rushed out of the car. "Mi appreciate yuh coming, but mi haffi deal wid dis now. Yuh unnastand?"

Terrence looked a bit disappointed but nodded. "Mi get it, Sienna. Jus' be careful, yeh?"

Sienna headed straight to Maria, the head of housekeeping at the B&B. The woman was well-known for being thorough and had a memory that missed nothing. "Maria, yuh hear anything 'bout a locket being found in one ah di empty rooms? "

Maria squinted, her eyes scanning the ceiling as she thought. Then, it clicked. "Ah yes, mi memba now. Summa di staff did a chat 'bout finding a locket inna one drawer. Mi think was Rachel or Lisa."

"Where dem deh now?" Sienna inquired, feeling a renewed sense of urgency.

"Mi think dem inna di laundry room now, sortin' linens," Maria replied, pointing down the hallway.

With a quick "Tanks, Maria," Sienna almost sprinted down the corridor to the laundry room. Her heart pounded in her chest. Each step felt like a tick-tock, counting down the time she had to make things right.

Bursting into the laundry room, she found Rachel and Lisa folding towels, their conversation paused by her sudden entrance.

"Mi sorry fi barge in soh," Sienna said breathlessly. "But either of yuh find a locket recently? Inna unoccupied room?"

Lisa looked down, visibly uncomfortable. She then turned a shade of beet-red.

"Lisa, where di locket deh now?" Sienna asked, her eyes narrowing.

Lisa stammered, "Mi... mi tek it to Jerome, di town jeweler. Mi tink seh nobody woulda miss it an' mi coulda get likkle money."

Sienna's eyes widened, her heart sinking for a moment before tightening into a fist of determination.

Sienna didn't have time to deal with Lisa's indiscretion. "Mi haffi go. No time fi waste." She bolted out of the laundry room, past a bewildered Maria, and rushed to find Terrence. Normally she'd walk the mile and a half to

Jerome's shop, but there was no time to waste.

"Mi need yuh fi drive mi to Jerome's, quick an' fast!" she told him.

Terrence didn't need further explanation. They got into his car, and he sped down the island roads, weaving past the usual island traffic. The urgency in Sienna's eyes told him everything he needed to know.

Pulling up in front of Jerome's shop, Sienna practically leapt out of the moving car. "Stay yah soh, mi soon come back," she called out to Terrence.

She dashed into the shop, beads of sweat on her forehead despite the shop's air-conditioning. Jerome, a middle-aged man with an eye for quality, looked up from his workbench.

"Mi looking for a locket, golden an' heart-shaped. Yuh have it?" Sienna blurted out, her words rushed and thick with urgency.

Leon squinted, then recognition flickered in his eyes. "Ah yes, a young lady brought dat in. Very peculiar piece, not dat expensive but intricate."

"Is it still yah?" Sienna felt like her entire world hinged on his next words.

Leon turned and opened a glass cabinet behind him. For what felt like an eternity, he sifted through various pieces of jewelry. Then he found it. He placed the small, golden, heart-shaped locket with its intricate designs on the counter.

Sienna felt like she could breathe again. "Mi need fi buy it, right now." She knew better than to go back and forth with Jerome about the origins of the locket and wanted to at least compensate him for his trouble.

As Jerome processed the transaction, Sienna felt a weight lift off her shoulders. She had the locket; she had a bargaining chip. Whoever was threatening Darren would have to deal with her now. She thanked Jerome, grabbed the locket, and sprinted back to the car where Terrence was waiting.

"It's time fi end dis," she whispered to herself, clutching the locket tightly in her hand as Terrence sped away.

35

Sienna's thoughts were a swirling storm as she returned to the B&B, the locket's weight heavy in her pocket. Terrence pulled up to the front entrance in his SUV, his eyes meeting hers in the rearview mirror. "Yuh need help, Sienna?" he offered, a hopeful note in his voice. Sienna couldn't afford distractions, though, not with whatF was at stake.

"Mi good, Terrence. Tanks," she said abruptly, offering a quick smile that didn't quite reach her eyes. She swung the car door open and stepped out, her heels crunching on the gravel driveway. Terrence watched her walk away, a mixture of concern and disappointment clouding his features.

As Sienna entered her cottage, her eyes swept the room before settling on the desk that doubled as her workstation. This was her sanctuary, a place where she pieced together clues and solved puzzles. With a determined stride, she walked over to the desk, pulling out her well-worn magnifying glass. Her analytical brain knew there was something she had to do first. Something so seemingly cheap, albeit intricately designed, shouldn't have put Darren at the brink of death. The locket shimmered as she placed it under the lens, its intricacies glowing under the focused beam of her desk lamp.

Just as she leaned in closer to examine the delicate patterns etched into the golden surface, her fingers betrayed her. The locket slipped, tumbling down onto the hardwood floor below. When it hit the ground, the clasp that kept the heart-shaped pieces together sprung open, revealing something she hadn't expected: a tiny micro drive embedded in the inner chamber.

Her eyes widened, a torrent of implications rushing through her mind. This was no mere trinket; it was a vessel for something far more significant. No wonder Darren had been beaten and left for dead! This locket was far more valuable than its external appearance would suggest.

Sienna carefully picked up the micro drive and walked over to a corner of the cottage where a tall structure stood, draped with a large velvet curtain. She pulled off the curtain to reveal a peculiar-looking laptop. It was encased in a metal grid—a homemade Faraday cage she had built during one of her criminology courses. The cage would ensure that whatever was on this drive would not infect her local network or tip off anyone that it was being accessed.

She opened the cage to the shielded laptop and plugged in the micro drive. Her fingers danced across the keyboard, running a series of security protocols. She was operating in a vacuum, digitally speaking; the Faraday cage ensured her actions were invisible to the outside world.

The files began to load, and Sienna braced herself. She was about to dive into information that someone had deemed worth inflicting bodily harm to protect. As the data appeared on her screen, she took a deep breath. The next few minutes could very well dictate how the rest of this dangerous chess game would unfold.

Sienna's eyes flickered across the screen as lines of zeros and ones populated the display. For a moment, she felt puzzled. Was this some form of encryption? But as she looked closer, a sudden realization washed over her: these were not just any zeros and ones; this was a Bitcoin private key.

Her hands trembling just slightly, Sienna moved the cursor to a separate window and initiated her custom Bitcoin script. The code she had written herself began to churn through the cryptographic computations, cross-referencing the private key with the blockchain. The screen flickered, and then the numbers popped up:

$1,000,000,000. One billion U.S. dollars in Bitcoin.

She let out an involuntary whistle, her body rigid with disbelief and a newfound sense of gravity. It wasn't just corporate secrets or some encrypted message; it was a digital fortune, one large enough to prompt unimaginable measures to protect it. Darren was nearly killed not for an ordinary locket—he was holding a billion-dollar fortune.

This revelation eclipsed everything she had thought before. Her original plan, confrontational and righteous, was now impossibly risky. Facing people desperate enough to protect a billion-dollar secret meant entering a game she couldn't afford to lose. The locket was not just a bargaining chip; it was a ticking time bomb.

Sienna sank into her chair, her eyes locked onto the glowing screen but seeing beyond it, into the myriad scenarios that could unfold. She had in her possession something that could set the entire island ablaze with danger. As she sat in her cottage, isolated from the world by her Faraday cage but intimately connected to an unimaginable web of risk, she had to decide her next move. And with a billion dollars and multiple lives in the balance, she knew that move had to be both extraordinarily cautious and impeccably smart.

Sienna clenched her fists, taking a deep, steadying breath. A billion dollars was motivation for all sorts of madness and mayhem. She needed help, but who could she trust? Law enforcement could be compromised; this was big money and big risks.

The locket buzzed in her hand as if echoing her thoughts—a digital Pandora's Box she had no idea how to close. But then it hit her: the only way to neutralize the threat was to move the money, make it inaccessible to those who sought it. With her secure setup, she could transfer the funds to a temporary holding wallet, rendering the locket useless to the assailants.

Taking another deep breath, Sienna began the process, typing lines of code with a sort of grim determination. Her script ran smoothly, and within minutes, she had moved the Bitcoin to a new wallet. She exhaled, not realizing she had been holding her breath.

Sienna took a few minutes to concoct a plan, scribbling it down on paper to help organize her thoughts. She needed to confront the mysterious couple, but not before alerting someone she could trust about the situation—in case things went awry. Uncle Lando, her favorite uncle and amateur sleuth, would be that person.

Sienna left her cottage and walked briskly toward the meeting point, feeling the locket in her pocket with each step. It was lighter now, devoid of its digital payload, but heavy with implications. Her phone had buzzed a few minutes earlier—Uncle Lando had agreed to meet her, and a flood of relief washed over her. If there was anyone who could help her navigate this high-stakes maze, it was Uncle Lando.

Reaching the designated spot, she found Uncle Lando already waiting. The man had always looked more like a cozy scholar than a shrewd accountant, his eyes perpetually twinkling behind his glasses. But Sienna knew better. She'd seen him maneuver through complex financial puzzles with the same ease that most people worked through a Sunday crossword.

"Ah, Sienna, mi love. Yuh look troubled," Uncle Lando observed as she approached.

She wasted no time in narrating her story, concluding with the staggering sum hidden in the locket. As she spoke, Uncle Lando's eyes narrowed, not in disbelief but in focused calculation.

"So yuh tek out di Bitcoin, all one billion dollars' worth?" he finally asked, his voice steady.

"Yes, it's secure—for now. Mi nuh know if dat make tings better or worse," she replied.

"Mi girl, yuh just find yuhself at di center of a very dangerous game," he said, his tone tinged with both concern and a certain professional fascination. "But di advantage yuh hold, ah dat di key to dis game is now in yuh hands, liter'ly."

"Yuh think we could trace it?" Sienna asked.

Uncle Lando grinned. "Yuh ask di right man, yuh know. Mi cyaan promise anyting, but we cyan try to fi find out where di money suppose to go. An' den, we mek our move."

Sienna sighed in relief. With Uncle Lando on her side, the odds felt a little less overwhelming. She had the currency, and now she had the means to possibly trace its destination. She wasn't alone in this whirlwind of chaos; she had an ally, one who understood the deadly interplay of money and danger.

36

For the first time since this ordeal began, Sienna felt they might just stand a chance. With her hand still gripping the empty locket, she prepared to dive deeper into this perilous labyrinth, but now with Uncle Lando to help her navigate its treacherous turns.

Uncle Lando and Sienna headed back to his office at the B&B, a room filled with an eclectic mix of tax manuals, financial texts, and a top-of-the-line computer setup. He worked for some of the island's wealthiest clients prior to switching to the B&B full-time, managing their portfolios and sometimes, their secrets.

"Mi gonna need yuh fi transfer di Bitcoin to a secure location mi control," he said as he booted up one of his encrypted laptops.

Sienna nodded and followed his lead. Moments later, they had moved the enormous digital fortune into a wallet Uncle Lando assured her was untraceable.

"Next, mi will try fi track di origin or at least find out who di money belong to," he said, his fingers deftly moving across the keyboard.

They worked in tense silence, punctuated only by the whirring of the computer's cooling fan and the sporadic clicks of the mouse. After what seemed like an eternity but was probably only minutes, Uncle Lando's eyes widened.

"Sienna, mi find sump'n yuh not gonna believe," he said, turning the screen toward her.

On it was an account name and a series of transactions linking back to an offshore account, one that was notorious for being used by an international cartel.

"Dis isn't just about money, Sienna. Dis is about power, control... an' obviously, dem willing fi kill fah it," Uncle Lando said, a shiver of realization running down his spine.

Sienna felt the weight of their discovery sink in. "Uncle Lando, we need fi involve di authorities, don't we?"

He nodded gravely. "But careful nuh. Yuh know how dis ting go. We need concrete evidence an' assurance dat di authorities not compromised."

Sienna took a deep breath. Her next steps would be precarious, each move carrying potential life-or-death consequences. But for the first time, she had something more powerful than fear: information. And with Uncle Lando's financial acumen and her own investigative skills, they had a fighting chance to turn the tables.

"Alright, Uncle Lando, let's bring dese people to justice. Dem pick di wrong island and people fi mess wid."

The two shared a determined nod, solidifying their newfound alliance against the ominous shadow that had fallen over their island. They would dive deeper into the web of corruption, armed with their wits and the billion-dollar secret now under their control.

Knowing they had to act fast, Uncle Lando started drafting an anonymous tip to Interpol. With his knowledge of financial systems, he could submit the tip in a way that wouldn't be traced back to them but would still be taken seriously.

"Mi just sent it. It's outta wi hands fah now," Uncle Lando said, exhaling deeply.

Sienna felt her phone buzz. It was a message from Darren: "Going home soon. Where are you?"

She replied quickly, letting him know she was safe and would explain everything later. But before she could put her phone away, it buzzed again.

This time it was from Sheryl: "Mi av eyes pon di criminal couple dem. Dem a act nervas, pacing inna dem room. A wha you wan mi fi do?"

Sienna looked at Uncle Lando, "Uncle, mi tink she it's time fi confront these people. But first, please mek sure seh di family nuh inna danger. Unnu cyan notify someone inna di police station yuh trust?"

"Mi know just di person," Uncle Lando said, picking up his phone to make a discreet call.

Sienna texted back Sheryl: "Keep yuh eye pon dem but nuh let dem see. Mi soon come."

She then called her parents, carefully selecting her words to not raise too much alarm but to alert them that they needed to be cautious. "Mumma, Puppa, mek sure di B&B it lock up tight tonight, okay? An' keep an eye on Darren. Im she im ready fi go home, but mi feel she, im mus stay inna di hospital for safety."

Her parents agreed, sensing the urgency in her voice but not questioning it for now.

Sienna felt the weight of the situation settle in. This was the point of no return. She had to balance the safety of her family, her concern for Darren, and the weighty knowledge she now carried.

37

As she stepped out of the B&B, with a singular dangerous plan in mind, Terrence was waiting there. "Yuh sure yuh nuh need mi help, Sienna? Yuh a run from ahso to dehso. Unnu mus be tired an need assistance."

She paused, contemplating. Normally, she'd decline, but today was different. "Actually, Terrence, I might. Just follow my lead and don't ask too many questions."

Terrence nodded, eager but visibly aware that this was no ordinary situation. "Lead di way."

Sienna, Terrence, and a hidden but compelling sense of justice behind them, set off to confront the British couple, uncertain of what they would find but armed with information that could bring down even the most dangerous of adversaries. They were staying at one of the standalone cottages at the B&B and for once, Sienna couldn't have been more grateful of their distance away from the main building, the family, and other guests.

Sienna and Terrence arrive at the secluded cottage where the infamous couple is staying. It's the perfect backdrop for a confrontation without attracting too much attention. Uncle Lando texted her moments before: "Police on standby. Mek sure she yuh clear a di area."

Of course, Sienna had made a glaring omission when sharing her plan with Uncle Lando: that she planned to confront the couple. She told him she was going to get irrefutable proof of their misdeeds but left out the part where it entailed coming face to face with them.

Terrence senses the tension, "Yuh alright, Sienna?"

"Ah'm nervous but ready," Sienna replies.

Taking a deep breath, Sienna knocks on the door. The man opens it, visibly surprised. "How can I help you?" he says, with an unmistakable British accent.

Sienna locks eyes with him. "Ah believe yuh missing sump'n important," she says, discretely showing him a photo of the locket on her phone.

The color drains from his face. "I—I don't know what you're talking about."

His wife appears behind him, eyeing Sienna and Terrence suspiciously. "Who are these people, Henry?"

Sienna switches her gaze to the woman. "We know 'bout di locket an' what's inside a it. It's over."

The woman looks horrified, then furious. "You have no idea who you're messing with."

"Actually, mi do," Sienna says, pulling out her phone again, this time showing a screenshot of the anonymous tip confirmation from Interpol. "An' now, so do the authorities."

Just as Sienna thought she had everything under control, Henry's expression changes to one of cold calculation. In a quick, fluid motion, he pulls a gun from behind his back, aiming it at Sienna and Terrence.

"Tut, tut," he says, as he motions them inside. "I believe you'll be letting us go on our merry way if you want to make it out of this alive," Henry sneers.

The woman quickly grabs a briefcase from the room, her eyes never leaving Sienna's.

Sienna gives a frightened nod, the heavy weight of what's happening pressing down on her. The couple back out of the room, Henry's gun still trained on them until they're safely out the door.

Within moments, they hear the sounds of police sirens wailing in the distance, but it's too late. An island local who's part of Uncle Lando's network calls in: "Dem jus' hit de marina, an' dem boardin' a speedboat!"

Sienna feels her heart sink as she and Terrence rush to the marina, just in time to see a speedboat roar to life and cut across the blue waters, getting farther and farther away. They've escaped, at least for now, and the gravity of the situation hangs heavily in the air.

Uncle Lando's text comes in: "Don' worry, mi niece. We'll catch dem."

Sienna looks at the horizon, then back at Terrence. "Ah don' know 'bout dat," she mutters, a heavy mix of relief and frustration settling within her. "But ah do know dis ain't di end."

38

Sienna and Terrence are escorted to the local police station, where they're led into an unassuming room with a metal table and a couple of chairs. The head detective, a tall man named Detective Roberts with greying temples and a stern demeanor, sits across from them.

"Alright, Sienna, Terrence, ah know dis ain't yuh firs' rodeo wit' troubleshootin', but dis one different. It deepah dan yuh think," he begins, shuffling some papers in front of him.

After going through a barrage of questions—everything from how they came into contact with the mysterious couple to their knowledge of the locket and the Bitcoin—it's clear Detective Roberts is evaluating not just their words, but their reactions.

"Ah've known 'bout yuh little investigashun skills, Sienna. Ah nevah interfere 'cause yuh nevah step on me toes. But dis one, dis a hole dif'rent beast," he says, leaning back in his chair.

"Yuh mean 'bout de Bitcoin, right? An' de locket?" Sienna inquires, her eyes narrowing.

Detective Roberts hesitates, glancing at Terrence before he continues, "Dat couple yuh met? Dem well known inna crime circles. Nuhbody nuh seh dem real names, so dem jus a call dem Di Smiths. Dem was 'ere to finalize a billion-dollar deal wit' a cartel dat's been creepin' up inna Jamaica. Wit'out dat money, dem inna hot watah. Dem haffi run 'cause de cartel tink dem do a double-cross."

Sienna coulds scarcely believe what she was hearing. What started as a local mystery erupted into an international crisis with dangerous players. The stakes were unimaginably high, and the chaos at the B&B was just the tip of the iceberg.

Detective Roberts leans in closer, locking eyes with Sienna, "Listen carefully, Sienna. We got one chance to get dis right, one chance to get dem an' protect de island. Yuh in?"

Sienna hesitates only for a second before nodding. "Ah in, Detective. Let's do dis."

Detective Roberts shuffles some papers aside and leans back in his chair, creating a momentary pause that seems to amplify the weight of what he's about to say. He locks eyes with Sienna, dismissing Terrence from the interrogation room with a glance and a nod.

Once Terrence closes the door behind him, he leans in close and says, "Sienna, dere's a task force. A special unit. Dem mobilize jus' fi take down dis cartel an' dis infamous couple yuh run into, di Smiths. Dem de top priority right now," he says, his tone taking on an even graver note.

Sienna feels her heartbeat quicken. She's crossed the boundary from local sleuth to something far more dangerous and far-reaching.

Detective Roberts continues, "Due to what yuh manage fi do in such a short time—recoverin' a billion dollars in stolen Bitcoin an' all—yuh've got di task force's attenshun. Dem invitin' yuh fi join dem as a consultant."

Her eyes widen at the offer, a mix of surprise, dread, and excitement filling her. In a split second, she thinks about her family, her community, and the B&B—her entire life is on this island.

Detective Roberts interrupts her thoughts, "Ah know yuh got yuh roots deep 'ere, but dis nuh jus bout us anymore. Yuh av a chance fi make a real dif'rence, globally. Oh, an' one more ting: di task force inna New York City."

The room falls silent. The bustling streets of New York feel like a world away from the sandy beaches and tight-knit community of her island. Yet, here she is, on the cusp of something bigger than she'd ever imagined.

"Ah've got family an' a life 'ere, Detective," she finally says, breaking the silence.

"Ah know, Sienna. But consider dis: how many lives yuh could save if yuh help bring down dis cartel and di Smiths? How much safer will di community be? Yuh got a gift, an' maybe it time fi use it on a biggah stage," Detective Roberts urges, his eyes full of sincerity.

Sienna takes a deep breath, mulling over the detective's words. The decision before her is enormous, one that could change the trajectory of her life forever.

"Ah need some time fi think 'bout it," she says.

"Of course, take all di time yuh need to tink it ovah tonight. But know dis, yuh've already proven yuhself in ways most people could a jus dream of," Detective Roberts replies, nodding in a gesture of deep respect.

As she leaves the station, the sun dipping low on the horizon, Sienna's mind is a swirl of conflicting emotions and ponderous thoughts. Her island, her family, and her community have shaped her into who she is, but now a larger world is calling, offering her a role in a drama of international proportions.

And for the first time, she's considering answering that call.

39

Sienna gathers her family in the grand hall of the B&B, her nerves almost palpable. The atmosphere is thick with tension as everyone settles in. She takes a deep breath before speaking.

"Mi got some news. Mi been offered a chance to join a task force in New York City. It big, mi know, but it could make a real difference," she reveals, her eyes scanning each family member's face.

Her mother looks as if she's been slapped, her eyes welling up. Puppa's jaw tightens, and he lets out a long sigh. Marley, her older sister, is the first to break the silence.

"Yuh cyaan be serious, Sienna. Yuh a go lef di family business, lef yuh home, fi what? Some dangerous job inna foreign?"

Her mother nods in agreement, "Mi cyan believe yuh would even consider dis, Sienna. We built dis business as a family. Yuh belong 'ere."

Puppa looks at his daughter, disappointment clouding his eyes. "Yuh always had a wild spirit but dis too much."

Sienna feels like she's been punched in the gut. She wasn't expecting unanimous support, but the outright opposition from her parents and Marley stung beyond words.

Then Lily, her younger sister, speaks up, "Hold on now, a mek unnu not even considering ar side? Sienna smart an capable. If she feel dis a her path, we should support her."

Uncle Lando chimes in, "a tru, Lily. Yuh have a gift, Sienna, one dat cyaan be wasted. Yuh could a help a lot of people. It a difficult decision, but it yuh decision to make."

Auntie Faye nods, adding, "Sometimes opportunities come once in a lifetime.

Mi think yuh should take it, even if it hard fi us to see you go."

The room falls into a hush, the lines clearly drawn. Sienna knows she's at a crossroads, her family on either side, her future uncertain.

She takes a deep breath, looks at each of them in turn, and says, "Mi made mi decision."

The room goes still, everyone's eyes on Sienna, waiting, their breaths held.

And just as she's about to speak, her phone buzzes with a message that makes her heart skip a beat. She reads it and looks up, her eyes filled with an emotion none of them can quite place.

"Something's come up," she says, her voice tinged with a gravity that wasn't there before. "Mi decision jus got a hole leap more complicated."

The room remains in a tense silence, the weight of her words hanging in the air, leaving everyone wondering what could possibly complicate things even more.

Sienna stares at her phone for a moment longer, the tension in the room almost unbearable. She looks up and locks eyes with her family, each of them still waiting, still caught in the suspended moment she's created.

"Mi sorry," she finally says, breaking the silence. "But mi haffi go. Dis a urgent."

Ignoring the confusion and concern etched on the faces around her, Sienna hurries out of the room, grabbing her bag and a light jacket as she goes. Puppa calls after her, but she's already out the door.

Her phone buzzes again as she steps into her car, the engine roaring to life. It's a message from Detective Roberts.

"Sienna, we av a lead on di Smiths dem. Di window is closing and you haffi leave tonight, so mi haffi know now. Yuh a go join?"

Her hands hover over the steering wheel, her heart pounding in her chest. She thinks about her family, about their home and the legacy they've built together. But then she thinks about the opportunity ahead, about right and wrong, justice and injustice, and what she can do to make a difference.

It's a defining moment, one that feels like it will shape the trajectory of her life. She takes a deep breath, steadies her hand, and types a single word in response.

"Yes."

As she speeds away from the only home she's ever known, Sienna feels a mix of dread and exhilaration. It's a new path, fraught with uncertainty and danger, but it's her path. And as she drives off into the night, toward an unknown future, she knows that there's no turning back.

Sienna Bailey and the Case of the Sinister Smiths

Just when Sienna Bailey thought she'd seen it all, a new message throws her life into uncharted territory. In *Sienna Bailey and the Case of the Sinister Smiths*, Sienna faces a choice that will forever alter her path. Leaving behind her family's legacy, the idyllic island, and the B&B that has been her world, she plunges into the labyrinthine streets of New York City. Joining a specialized task force, she is thrust into an operation that zeroes in on the notorious Smiths, a criminal syndicate with tendrils reaching far beyond the Big Apple.

As Sienna navigates betrayal, secrets, and a new set of rules, she must decipher who she can trust in a world that seems to offer anything but clarity. The hunt for the Smiths pulls her into a web of organized crime, political corruption, and dark secrets, challenging Sienna in ways she never imagined. In a city that never sleeps, neither does evil—and it's up to Sienna

Bailey to ensure justice prevails. Prepare yourself for a gripping story of courage, dilemma, and unshakeable resolve. Are you ready for Sienna's next thrilling case?

www.ingramcontent.com/pod-product-compliance
Lightning Source LLC
Chambersburg PA
CBHW031948240626
47153CB00003B/909